A SOLDIER AT WAR:

The World War II Letters of Borys Bohun

JAMES BOHUN

ERSTUN PRESS

ISBN 979-8-9897653-2-4 (print)
ISBN 979-8-9897653-3-1 (eBook)

CONTENTS

PREFACE

While in high school, I received a class assignment: students were required to ask one parent about life during the Great Depression and the Second World War. My father provided me with information about his service in the United States Army and the Civilian Conservation Corps. He was quite open about his experiences on this occasion, whereas he rarely spoke of his military service. This stimulated my interest in WWII, and I read books, magazines, and watched films on the subject.

After my father's death, my mother gave me the letters he wrote during his overseas service, and she answered questions I raised while reading the letters. She also informed me of her 1943 Valentine's Day letter that Borys highly valued. From the information she provided, I rebuilt that cherished correspondence. The love and optimism expressed by Borys inspired me with a desire to share his positive attributes with the reader.

Additionally, the writings from my father provide insight into changes in American wartime social structure as viewed by ordinary people. Topics such as submarine warfare, rationing, and war production are discussed. This manuscript is intended to be a highly readable account of Borys Bohun's war experience seen through his letters home.

During the first decade of this century, I was honored with membership in the 62nd Anti-Aircraft Artillery Battalion Association, consisting of survivors of that World War II unit. During my tenure, I gathered information through telephone interviews, personal histories, and photos. I also obtained a copy of *The War Diary of the 62nd Anti-Aircraft Artillery (AAA) Gun Battalion* and used this primary source document to determine the dates and locations of the battalion during the war. World War II terminology was used in this book, including the names of cities and nations during the conflict.

I have purposely retained the grammatical and spelling errors in Borys's letters. Redundant information, written in three or four letters to ensure Martha would get at least one, was removed after its first use. Other omissions include the letters' greetings to Martha's family members asking how they were, and the closings giving his regards, blessings, and wishes for good health to all family members. Ellipses are used to indicate where a passage has been omitted; these sections usually contain personal information, and their removal does not change the content of the letter.

PART ONE:

NORTH AFRICA

1

November 1942

Oran, Algeria

Twenty-four-year-old Private First Class Borys Bohun was among the American troops who marched to their army camp from a landing ship in Oran Harbor, Algeria. This port and others in Morocco and Algeria were captured after three days of intensive battle in early November 1942. The offensive in North Africa was the first great Allied military effort against European Fascism.

Along the march, Borys constantly thought of his fiancée, Martha Boretsky. They shared the same facial characteristics of blue eyes and brown hair. Martha filled the void in Borys's life that he had in early adulthood. Without Martha, his life was empty of the love and happiness she provided him. He hoped she would receive the letter he had written aboard the troop transport, and she eventually did:

My Dearest Martha,

Please forgive the writing and paper because it's the best I could get and it's slightly hard to write on board ship.

I've left England and am now somewhere on the ocean going somewhere and don't know until we reach our destination. I don't know when and if you'll receive this letter, so I pray if this letter gets to you it finds you and everybody back there well and happy. Martha darling, I'm asking you to write my folks if you receive this letter and let them know I'm well and have left England. Please explain I've only had one stamp [air mail] and had quite a job getting it.

... I don't expect you to stay home every night because it isn't fair to you to be miserable and worried. You can have a good time and still be true to me, ... when I get back to marry you then we'll both stay home and settle down with Patrica. [Martha and Borys previously agreed to that name for their first child.] I can only look forward to one thing and that is to be with you and married to you.

Regardless of what you think or say, I'm the luckiest guy in the world to have a girl like you, and I'd give anything I could ever have to be with you right now and see and hold you once again for that minute, but if everything turns out the way I'm hoping I'll be with you once more, only this time it'll be for good, Okay Mrs. Bohun....

Give my regards and love to everybody, especially to my wife Martha and don't forget to tell Martha that I love her ever so much and tell her I think she's the sweetest girl in the world and I love my girl/wife Martha... when I kiss her, Oh Boy she just makes me go dizzy with love and aside all that she's the sweetest girl I've ever met and the only girl I've ever honestly could or ever love.

Always remember darling I'll always love you and will try to be a good husband when that lucky day comes. Am now closing.

God bless your sweet heart Darling and every body back home.

Loving You Forever,

Borys

Borys was an industrious youth, a trait he inherited from his parents, who emigrated from a part of the Austrian-Hungarian Empire in Eastern Europe and became naturalized American citizens. His name was misspelled on his birth certificate. As one of the oldest of nine children, he performed menial jobs to earn a few cents, a necessity during the 1930s Depression since his family lived in poverty, like tens of millions of other Americans. One of his favorite tasks was to go summer blueberry picking with his father in the woods. They would gather buckets of blueberries and sell them to local bakers; his mother also made blueberry pierogi and pies.

Borys dropped out of high school after the eleventh grade to work for the Civilian Conservation Corps (CCC), a government-funded program, so his family could have some income. He made thirty dollars a month and was required to send twenty-five home; he sent twenty-seven or twenty-eight bucks a month and kept the other couple dollars for personal items such as soap and candy.

While in the CCC, Borys performed duties as a lumberjack in the Oregon wilderness, thousands of miles from his home in Fall River, Massachusetts, a textile-producing city also known for the 1890s gruesome axe murders of Lizzie Borden's parents. He worked on forestry projects, such as flood control, and built firebreaks to help control forest fires. Borys's ruddy complexion laid testament to the strenuous outdoor labor he had done the past several years.

Borys, whose nickname was Butch, had been in the Army Coast Artillery three years before the war, beginning in August 1938. His enlistment had come up two months before the 7 December 1941 unprovoked Japanese bombing of Pearl Harbor, Hawaii. That was the peacetime army, and Borys had never been in combat.

After his military service, Borys returned to Fall River and obtained a well-paying defense industry job but gave that up to reenlist in the army after the Japanese attack on US Armed Forces. Now that he was in the army again and had met Martha in Brooklyn, New York, during March 1942, Borys's greatest fear was that he would never return home and unite with her if the worst happened.

As a member of one of Battery C's 90-mm gun crews, part of the 62nd Coast Artillery Antiaircraft Regiment (AAA), Borys and the rest of the team performed the back-breaking task of digging their nearly ten-ton gun into a tactical position for defense of the Port of Oran against Axis aerial attack. Having the cannon's platform in the earth provided stability when it was fired. Additionally, protective revetments (i.e., barricades or walls) consisting of sandbags surrounded their position.

The sky was quiet the first week that the 62nd AAA occupied Oran. Suddenly, at 2042 hours on the night of 22 November 1942, an air raid alert sounded. All antiaircraft batteries engaged unseen aircraft with radar control at 2050 hours.

Antiaircraft artillery shells ineffectively hunted hostile aircraft over Oran that night, even as the searchlight battalion explored the gloomy sky to illuminate an enemy target. The conflict heightened when .50-caliber machine guns and 40-mm guns joined the fight. Their tracer ammunition could be seen rummaging around the heavens, unsuccessfully searching for their foe. No claims of destroyed or damaged enemy aircraft were made on 22 November 1942. The raid was turned away, with no damage inflicted on the port. When the firing ceased, all eyes watched the sky, lit by the glow of a full moon, until the all-clear sounded at 2320 hours.

As dawn broke the following morning, Borys washed up, taking care to attend to a hand injury he received the previous night while loading artillery shells. He wrote to his fiancée:

My Dearest Martha,

I am writing this letter hoping it finds you well and happy. I can't write well because the thumb of my right hand is cut, and is healing fast. How are you sweetheart? Write as soon as possible and let me know how things are.

How is your Mom & Dad, Pete, Jim [Martha's brothers-in-law], Anne, Mary, Lizzie [Martha's sisters], & your brothers Johnny, George, & Mike? Give them all my regards & give your Mom & Dad my Love.

Do you write or receive any letters from my home? Please let me know... Do you receive mail from my brothers Andy or Teddy?

Am praying you received all my mail and this letter. Haven't received but 2 letters from you [while in Great Britain] and know your mail is somewhere and will eventually get to me. I hope you understand Martha Darling if you don't receive mail from me because there is so much work in finding and assorting mail before it gets to me or perhaps you. Even if you don't receive mail from me or if I don't get mail from you Darling, we always know regardless of anything we'll be together someday....

The first letter Borys received from Martha while in Great Britain was on 5 October 1942, which she sent via air mail on 21 September 1942; it took two weeks! In his response, the same day he received the letter, Borys wrote, "I'm about the happiest fellow in the world after receiving your letter and reading it. I've read it about a dozen times and am still reading it..." He continued, "I haven't received your other 2 letters yet, but imagine I'll get them sometimes because it takes quite a while for ordinary 3 cent postage."

I'm glad to hear Mary will have a blessed event and do hope it'll be on the luckiest day of our lives <u>Mar. 25</u>. I'll never forget that date because I've met the sweetest girl in the world, <u>my future wife</u> and <u>darling</u> on that lucky day. You're going to be a <u>sweet</u> & <u>pretty wife</u> and I'm going to work hard because I <u>love</u> you....

Tell Mary and Jim I hope it's a boy. Our first one will be a girl (Patrica). Gee honey, when that day comes, I'll get so swell headed I'll get top heavy....

Gee Martha Darling, I miss you, but in time I know we'll be together bound by our love & marriage. You're the only person I can and the only girl I could ever love as I do... Will you marry me after this is all over darling? [Meaning at the war's end; they were already engaged.]...

It's hard to say when we get paid, but I'll try my best to send money whenever possible. I'll try to send as much as possible because we can have a little for our future, just as we planned.... I'm going to have my mother send you $30.00 every month. Let me know if my mother has received the allotment yet. If you visit my sister [Sue in Brooklyn, NY] or aunt tell them I'm getting along fine....

At present I'm now in <u>Africa</u>...

Tell Johnny even though I'm a Pvt. we've all had it pretty tough since we've left the good old U.S.A. and it really isn't a cinch or a picnic over here and only when we go through it and see it do we realize <u>War</u> is really a living hell and the people of the U.S.A. really do have it good over there....

Is it possible for you to send me a tooth brush and razor blades and some soap? I could always use it, because it's pretty hard to get certain things here.

If you receive mail from me, write and let my folks know about it because sometimes it may be hard to write....

Tell your mom she'll have to put up with a son in law that likes to drink coffee and likes to talk a lot at the table, so she'll have plenty of company....

The nights and days are awfully lonesome without you and when I get back don't blame me if I squeeze you too hard and kiss you until I run out of breath.

Martha darling I'm closing with all my sincerest love hoping this letter reaches and finds you in the best of health with regards and love to everybody.

Ever lasting Love,

Borys   XXXXX ♥ XXXXX ♥ XXXXX ♥ XXXXX ♥ XXXXX

In addition to letters, GIs and civilians sent one-page V••• — Mail, usually written as V-mail. The three dots and a dash were Morse code for the alphabet letter "V," which was the Allies' symbol for "Victory." Some V-mail was microfilmed in batches, and the film was sent to the US for restoration. It was then mailed to the intended recipient, such as the letter from Borys to Martha reproduced below (actual size four and an eighth inches by five and an eighth inches), complete with the Censors Stamp in the upper left-hand corner.

No. 669564

CENSORS STAMP

Miss Martha Boretsky
1517 – 11th Ave.
Brooklyn, N.Y.
U.S.A.

SENDERS NAME — P.F.C. Borys Bohun
SENDERS ADDRESS — Btry C 62nd CA AA
A.P.O. 302 %Postmaster
New York City, N.Y.
DATE — Sept. 24, 1943

Dearest Beloved Martha,

Hoping you are able to read my writing and hope you received previous letters. Am in the best of spirits and health. I'm looking forward to receiving mail from you soon sweetheart and am waiting in suspense. Will keep correspondence as much as possible. Am thanking your Mom, Dad, Anne, Mary, Pete and Jim for the hospitality they've shown me, and will repay that hospitality when we're together again. Thinking of you constantly and feel you next to me just as if we were together. Give my regards and love to everybody. Keep your chin up sweetheart and I'll be with you sooner than we expect. Loving you more than ever. God Bless You All. xxxx Ever Lasting Love, Borys xxx

Borys didn't complain to Martha about the specifics of the living conditions he and other GIs had to endure. Everyone had a beef about sleeping on the ground in their pup tents with no bedding other than a bedroll filled with straw. No matter how carefully a soldier filled the bedroll, some insects would always get in and crawl out nightly to feast on its victim. Additionally, the ground was cold and hard, even with the straw to insulate and cushion the soldier. Although the regiment was bivouacked in the desert, the temperature always plummeted at night. The desert rats were particularly bother-some and would sneak under the tent and gnaw on a soldier's belongings if he was lucky; otherwise, the GI would be awoken by the rat's bites. The troops were cautioned *not* to shoot the rats. The regiment's commanding officer was worried a sleeping GI would become an innocent victim of a misplaced shot. Men were encouraged to either beat the rodent with a rifle butt or use their bayonet.

Soldiers missed other comforts of home, such as entertainment and sports. As November neared its close, Borys and another artilleryman, Kevin Lake, talked about the previous month's World Series. Lake, a Brooklyn boy, and fan of the Dodgers, was upset since the Yankees had made it to the 1942 World Series and the Brooklyn Dodgers hadn't.

"Don't feel so bad," Borys said. "Coming from Massachusetts, I'm a Red Sox fan. My fiancée, Martha, is a Yankees fan. Before I left her in New York back in the summer to go overseas, I bet her the Sox would beat the Yankees and win both the Pennant and the World Series. Now she won that bet because the Yanks took the 1942 American League Pennant. I have to pay her when I get home. And I tell you, I look forward to paying that bet."

"What did you bet her?" Lake asked.

"Twenty-five kisses for the Pennant and another twenty-five for the Series," Borys answered.

Borys regretted that he and Martha could not be together for their first Thanksgiving since meeting. He wrote her that he looked forward to Thanksgiving of the following year with Martha and her family—surely the war would end before then, and the troops would be home.

On Thanksgiving, 26 November, memorial services were held for the American and French army and navy personnel killed in the occupation on 8–10 November 1942.

One-third of a day's rations were distributed to French civilian and military personnel in the vicinity of each gun position, with an explanation as to the significance of Thanksgiving Day.

With the successful capture of Oran and Algiers and the surrender of French Vichy forces, the Allies moved east through Algeria and into western Tunisia. Their goal was to capture the seaports of Tunis and Bizerte in northeastern Tunisia to prevent Axis forces from transporting reinforcements.

German and Italian infantry, tankers, artillerymen, and support troops were rushed to Tunisia via sea and air from Italy, its large island of Sicily, and southern France.

Mid-November saw the first combined Allies (American, British, and Free French) and Axis (German and Italian) forces battle in Tunisia. By the end of November, hundreds of miles east of Oran, the Allies were almost within artillery range of Tunis, the capital of Tunisia, where Axis forces were poised to strike back at the Allies. Like other outfits, the 62nd AAA would make its way to Tunisia.

2

December 1942

Oran, Algeria

On 1 December 1942, the Germans began a counteroffensive to defend Tunis. Thus began protracted combat in North Africa involving American troops.

In England, Borys had received only two of Martha's letters in two months, although she had written at least once a week. It was the same with his family; they had sent weekly letters, and he had received only two in England and one in Africa. Borys wrote Martha and informed her that he had finally received three of her letters in Oran, the most recent dated 8 October.

> *My Dearest Darling Martha,*
>
> *Writing another letter from Africa, making my second from here and another I've written on my voyage to here. Was very happy to hear from you and am sending another kiss which is real. (X) It was a beautiful picture of everybody you sent and you were especially pretty Darling. Can you blame me for Loving you, Darling.*

Gee Darling, you look slightly worried in the picture, <u>please</u>
don't worry because I'll be back quicker than people think we'll be
back. Haven't as yet received any packages, but expect to get them
for <u>Christmas</u> any way.

Unbeknownst to the American people, hundreds of freighter and tanker ships had been sunk by German U-boats off the coast of the United States. These submarines had immense destructive capabilities and nearly inflected a crippling blow to Allied shipping in the early part of the war. In fact, 1942 saw over twice as many Americans killed by subs than by the attack on Pearl Harbor, which claimed the lives of over twenty-four hundred Americans.

Borys and other GIs, as well as millions of Americans, were not aware of the true sea terror—only part of the horror was reported in the press, that which was witnessed by civilians on shore or told by merchant seamen. He would not receive most of the packages sent during the last quarter of 1942 in time for Christmas, or ever. Instead, the recipient was the legendary seafaring Davy Jones, who tucked away millions of tons of cargo in his locker.

If this letter gets to you before my last letter, it will most likely be af-
ter Christmas any way, I'm wishing you all again,—had a very Mer-
ry Christmas and a Happy and a Prosperous New Years to come,
and again to you, <u>Sweetheart</u> <u>Darling</u>, I'm wishing the same hoping
and praying we'll spend the next one together with you Darling as
my wife. God Bless your sweet little heart.

It certainly is <u>swell</u> to receive all them <u>engagement</u> <u>presents</u>. I'll *get a job in N. Y. as soon as this war is over, and seeing you're boss you'll have to pick out where to live in. I don't care where I live as long as I <u>have you</u> to love & take care of <u>our Patrica</u>, and Darling, I do, and will love you forever....*

Growing up in Massachusetts with hard-working parents, the Puritan work ethic was firmly entrenched in Borys. He repeatedly expressed his intention to get a job and work hard in subsequent correspondence.

...tell me Darling in your next letter, <u>please</u>, where you'd like to spend <u>our honeymoon</u> and <u>where you</u> would like to live, because I'll try and will have every thing come out (<u>just</u>) the way you want it to.

I suppose I've said it a 1000 times I love & adore you so I'm going to make it <u>1001</u> and I only wish I could have you in my arms not only tonight but always for ever to keep telling you. Again I'm asking you <u>Sweetheart Darling</u> not to worry because I'm fine and well, and love you just as much and always will forever & ever....

Fell into luck and finally found your pictures and the Bible your mother gave me. It was quite a relief to receive my personal property shipped separately because it's the only things I have that are worth while.

The pictures we took at Coney Island bring memories of swell times we spent at the Island, especially the rides on the <u>cyclone</u>....

Borys and Martha in Coney Island, New York, summer 1942.

<u>Darling</u> I've met some people in Africa that are married and a man that is single. The couple that are married are French, both around the age of 50, and the other is Polish around the age of 40. They have a small place with 2 rooms and the 3 of them live there. They are swell people, very clean & respectable and have asked me & a buddy of mine to visit them, which we have on the <u>very</u>, <u>very</u> short time we get off once every ten days or so, which is only a matter of hours. My buddy and I go there to shave and take a <u>bath</u>, which is quite a luxury here when our time for our few hours off does come. They've given us what little food they have and treat us just as if we were their own sons. They have no children of their own. As long as we stay here we have a place to keep clean. They also wash our clothes for us, and we otherwise could never do it ourselves, because we are in the field. I told them of my future wife (<u>you Martha Darling</u>) and they send you their regards and give <u>us</u> (you & I) their best wishes & luck for a speedy reunion & marriage....

You've given me more happiness than I could ever want and I just am and will try to give you the same and <u>hope</u> I've done it just as long as I've known you.

Am now closing this letter with best regards to everybody back there and love to everybody, and to you darling, Love Again.

With All My Love Yours For Ever,
<u>Borys</u>   XXXXX ♥ XXXXX ♥ XXXXX ♥ XXXXX ♥ XXXXX

<u>Keep</u> the <u>coffee</u> pot <u>hot</u>. Take good care of your self Darling.

Eleven days before Christmas, Borys wrote a one-page letter to Martha that was immediately passed by the censor and shipped the same day by the US Army Postal Service. The outside of the envelope contained the words "Christmas Mail" in bold print. This was the army's procedure to assure their men that their loved ones would receive a "Christmas present" from the GI.

Borys wished Martha, her family, his family, and all their friends "A Merry Christmas"… "A Happy & Prosperous New Years to come with the Blessings of God to you all."

My Dearest Darling Martha,

Am writing this letter knowing it is a <u>special</u> <u>letter</u> and will get to you for <u>Christmas</u>. If you haven't received my other letters, I'm letting you know again I'm in Africa. I've only received 3 of your letters and 2 from home since I've been here and as yet no packages, but will eventually get to me. Can only write one sheet so am writing small. Let my folks know I'm well.

<u>I'll</u> <u>always</u> <u>will</u> <u>love</u> & <u>adore you</u> <u>darling</u> and the day will shortly come when I will call you my wife and we will also have our Patrica just as we planned. I pray we will be all together for next Christmas with <u>you</u> <u>sweetheart</u> <u>darling</u> as my wife.

Gee sweetheart Darling how I miss <u>you</u> & <u>your</u> <u>love</u> & I'd give (<u>anything</u>) to be just a few minutes with (<u>you Darling</u>) on Christmas Day. Relay my folks my sincerest Love. <u>Martha</u> <u>Darling</u> (<u>please</u>) if you ever need anything (<u>please</u>) use our money & get it, because I <u>expect</u> you to.

> *Gee <u>Darling</u> now that we got all them engagement presents we only have to buy the furniture for (<u>our</u>) home and we'll get that as soon as I get out of the army & I'll get a job right off & we'll get married. Darling I wish I could hold you in my arms and whisper my love for you.*
>
> *<u>Hoping</u> you had enough money to buy Christmas presents with. Get something nice for <u>Marys Baby</u> (<u>please Darling</u>.)*
>
> *Please don't worry if you don't receive my mail for long inter-vals, because even if you don't I'll be back to (<u>marry</u>) <u>Love</u> & adore <u>you</u> & <u>Patrica</u>.*
>
> *Have to close now with best of health regards & love to every-body. God Bless you All. With all <u>my Sincerest</u> & <u>devoted Love</u> to <u>you Martha sweetheart Darling</u>.*
>
> *<u>My Everlasting Love to You</u>,*
> *<u>Borys</u>   XXXXX ♥ XXXXX ♥ XXXXX ♥ XXXXX ♥ XXXXX*

On Christmas Eve, Borys received a letter from his parents dated 20 October, as well as a package. He also received a letter from his brother Ted, dated 14 November, with his baby's picture in it. Hours after Christmas, Borys wrote Martha informing her he received two of her letters on Christmas Day and, "I couldn't have received a better present than hearing <u>you</u> <u>loved</u> <u>me</u> on Christmas Day…" and "I was about the <u>happiest</u> man in the world."

The US Army used the procedure established for Thanksgiving the previous month. On Christmas morning, one-third of a day's rations were distributed to French civilian and military personnel in the vicinity of each gun position.

3

January 1943

Oran, Algeria

The new year brought mail, and more arrived during the month. Borys wrote to Martha in January 1943 and mentioned writing "V-letters" to Martha's siblings, as well as to his mom. He planned on writing his father, brothers and sisters, Sue, Pauline, Louise, and Helen, the last of whom Borys stated was "quite good at playing the violin."

My Dearest Darling Martha,

Here it is the beginning of a New Year, the year of <u>1943</u> <u>that</u> <u>I</u> <u>have</u> <u>promised</u> to be back to the sweetest girl, the girl of my life, the girl <u>I</u> <u>love</u> & <u>adore</u>, my near future wife (<u>You</u> <u>Martha</u> <u>Dearest</u>)... received Mary's Package and as yet haven't received yours & your Moms. I checked the items of the package with your letter & everything was there. Thank Mary for me, <u>Darling</u>.

<u>Martha</u> <u>Dearest</u> <u>Darling</u>, I'm about the happiest fellow in the world, after hearing from you, and I only wished I could tell you personally just how much your mail inspires me. <u>I</u> <u>love</u> <u>you</u>, <u>ever</u> & <u>ever</u> <u>so</u> <u>much</u>. Gee Darling, if only I knew you wanted to put your

arms around me on the <u>Cyclone</u>, I'd of never got off until they'd of closed for the night.

I can only say Martha Dearest, with you to help me & your love to inspire me, I'll work & work so that we can have our little Patrica and perhaps one or so more? It'll be just you & I Darling, raising our little family & loving each other, & giving our love to our Pat-rica and ...

In my other letters I asked you to send different things like candy, gum, soap, tooth paste which is very hard to get here, so if you get the chance Darling, please send it, because I'm bound to get them here. If I get them I can very well use it, if not Darling it will be worth the chance which you'd take <u>for</u> <u>me</u> <u>Darling</u>. Tell your teacher she'd be <u>most</u> <u>welcome</u> <u>at</u> <u>our</u> <u>wedding</u>, <u>Dearest</u> <u>Darling</u>. <u>It Hurts Me To Hear Of Things Being Rationed In The States</u>, and pray to God it won't be for long... I'll take that bet, I say Mary & Jim will have a baby boy, so you'd better prepare for them 25xxxxxxxxxxxxxxxxxxxxxxxxx Ask Mary if she recognizes the stationary & envelope I've written this letter on. It's hers, thank her again for me... Martha Dearest Darling, my love for you will always live, and I can only say if God will spare me through this war, I'll be back with you and will do my best to <u>give</u> <u>you</u> <u>happiness</u> as <u>my</u> <u>wife</u>....

Darling, I've just come to the conclusion, <u>no</u> <u>twin</u> <u>beds</u>. I'm pret-ty brave saying this, seeing you're not around. I'll tell you dearest, you'll have a hard job with me trying to get twin beds after we're married. Darling you can have anything else you ask for and can be <u>boss</u>, but the twin bed situation, I'll be the <u>big</u> (<u>boss</u>).

How is Augie [the nickname of Martha's brother, George] mak-

ing out with his schooling of parachuting? According to what I hear the rationing in the States is beginning to increase for different articles. My Mom tells me you write her regularly, <u>thanks</u> <u>Darling</u>....

I was rereading the diary you wrote while I was away in Long Island last summer. It was <u>swell</u> and that one part you said, I was branded in your life forever made me feel just as if you were next to me. <u>Dearest</u> you're also branded into my heart, soul, and life forever and ever.

Martha had made diary entries about her feelings toward Borys in early June 1942, before Borys had shipped out in August of that year. This was the time when he had been away from her since Battery C had temporarily been stationed at Riverhead, Long Island, for target practice and training. Battery C had returned to Brooklyn's Prospect Park the third week of June, just before Borys's marriage proposal to Martha on her birthday, 24 June 1942.

Every day I keep sweating out the mail to see if any letters from you have arrived. When I hear my name called, my heart begins to pound, hoping its from you <u>Darling</u>....

Darling, the kiss you sent me for New Years was the sweetest thing I could ever want and I've wore the lipstick off the paper and I'm still kissing it. <u>Please</u> <u>Darling</u>, send me one with every letter you write me, <u>please</u>. I haven't received your or your moms package yet, but it still may get to me, if not by the end of Feb. I believe they must be lost.

I'm writing this letter by a little kerosene light in the pup tent, and it's pretty hard to see, boy this little light smokes like the dickens. The poor guy that sleeps next to me has to put up with me. I keep him awake nights talking of you. Right now he's telling me, go ahead kiss the lipstick, (your kiss), don't mind me he says, and Darling I am kissing it I don't care if the world watches me....

Martha Darling, will you do me a favor, please. With the 400 or 500 pennies you've saved, will you get war stamps with the pennies, and when Patrica (our Patrica) has grown, we'll buy her a graduation dress when the time comes for her to graduate, with the war stamps you're now saving, and I'll tell her, your mom and I thought of this day and lived for this day when we were just a young loving couple.

Do you know the watch my pop gave me Darling, well the crystal fell off, the hands fell off but it's still running after I put it together again....

Darling, in my spare time I'm trying to figure different costs for a home and our marriage, and I've come to the conclusion that as soon as I get discharged from the army, I'll have to get a job as soon as possible. Darling, you'll have to take every penny of my pay, because I know you can save better than I can. Darling, by that I don't mean to say you're stingy. I'll give you an example if you remember at Coney Island we took a few pictures once and the woman could have talked me into taking anything, as long as I had the money, so you see what I mean Darling. You're not stingy, Dearest, you have good common sense so you're going to have to take care of all financial matters.

Loving you Martha sweetheart Darling with all my heart and soul forever and ever. God Bless you all.

Loving You Forever Only You,

Borys   XXXXX ♥ XXXXX ♥ XXXXX ♥ XXXXX ♥ XXXXX

The realization that some mail was not getting through became increasingly apparent. This was especially true with packages.

Initially, soldiers blamed the slow mail on the war or perhaps being misdirected and becoming "lost." Some theft could also have accounted for not receiving mail and packages, but the increasing suspicion was that the enemy was responsible for many undelivered items. The soldiers did not discuss this, as they feared it might be true; unfortunately, it was accurate, as submarine warfare was taking more of a toll. The U-boats had proved that stealth was an important battle element for surprise at sea, just like on land. Radar negated this concept somewhat and provided an early warning of an impending aerial attack. On 20 January 1943, antiaircraft defenses were alerted at 2015 hours. Batteries were fired on unseen aircraft with radar control fifty minutes later, and the all-clear sounded at 2202 hours. The size of the raid could not be determined; no aircraft were believed to have been shot down.

4

Fᴇʙʀᴜᴀʀʏ 1943

Oran and the Vicinity of Constantine, Algeria

Globally, February 1943 held both formidable encounters with Axis forces and great potential for the Allies. The details of these events were reported in newspapers, magazines, and on the radio, and the particulars reached Borys and other GIs.

Early February brought news that American forces achieved final victory on Guadalcanal in the Solomon Islands over the Japanese on 9 February 1943. This long-awaited triumph occurred after a six-month land, sea, and air struggle. This success not only stopped the Japanese advance in the South Pacific, it also protected American shipping lanes to Australia and the threat to that continent.

There was great news from Europe that our Soviet ally completely destroyed the German Sixth Army at Stalingrad (present-day Volgograd). This was truly significant since at least eighty percent of battle in Europe was on the eastern front, and the Russians were now on the offensive against Nazi forces.

The later part of February 1943 saw the first dismal defeat for US forces in the North African campaign. It happened at the Battle of Kasserine Pass, a series of battles during the ten days commencing Valentine's Day 1943 and culminating 23 February 1943. During the first week of conflict, US forces were pushed back from this strategic Tunisian pass. After their initial losses, American troops turned the tide of battle, and pushed the Axis enemy back with the aid of their British ally. The Allies were overtaking air superiority in North Africa that the Axis powers had held at the end of 1942. Over the next several months, air power would play a vital role in defeating the German and Italian air and ground forces.

The 62nd Coast Artillery Antiaircraft Regiment was given orders to move to a new location. Borys would no longer have the luxury of bathing with warm water or a home-cooked meal provided by the French couple once every ten days. It was back to eating cold food out of can. One consolation was that as long as the regiment was on the move, the GIs could heat their day's allotment of C rations before movement in the morning. They punched a small hole in the can's top to vent it and then put it in a basket near the truck's engine. The food would be hot by noon unless someone overlooked cutting the opening; then, the can would explode, resulting in a hungry soldier having to clean the engine.

At 0745 hours on 10 February 1943, the 62nd AAA Regiment movement by motor transportation to the Constantine, Algeria, area began. Tactical positions vacated around Oran were taken over by batteries of another antiaircraft artillery regiment. The difficult task of digging the 90-mm guns in the ground was made easy for the replacement outfit since trenches already existed.

Three-and-a-half days later, tactical positions were taken up near Constantine with the mission of defending B-17 bomber and P-38 fighter airfields. The 62nd AAA soldiers were back to the strenuous and labor-intensive work of excavating tons of dirt, stone, and other debris to dig in the Long Tom (nickname for the M1A1 90-mm gun) and fill sandbags.

After several days of settling in the new position, Borys wrote Martha, informing her he did not receive any of her January letters or packages or those sent by either of their mothers.

<u>My</u> <u>Own</u> <u>Dearest</u> <u>Darling</u> <u>Martha</u>,

<u>Martha</u> <u>Darling</u>, I think I'll start off by telling you what I've never told you before, that is <u>I</u> <u>love</u> <u>you</u> <u>ever</u> <u>and</u> <u>ever</u> <u>so</u> <u>much</u>...I remember the time I was at Camp Kilmer and we had a 20 mile hike, well I was just <u>dead</u> <u>tired</u>, so I called you up from camp to let you know I wasn't coming to see you that night. Ann answered the phone and I told her, but then when she told me you were sick, boy did I move out of that camp to see you. Nothing could have held me there. My heart was beating all the way until I got to you. Gee Darling, after I saw you in bed and talked to you and then we started to laugh, gee I wished I could express my <u>happiness</u> to see you laugh. You know Darling, <u>I</u> <u>wouldn't</u> have gone back to camp, if you weren't better....

It's been 165 days today that I've been away from you Martha Darling. It's the most miserable 165 days I've yet spent and yet <u>I'm</u> <u>happy</u> <u>knowing</u> <u>I</u> <u>have</u> <u>you</u> <u>and</u> <u>knowing</u> <u>you</u> <u>love</u> <u>me</u> <u>and</u> <u>are</u> <u>awaiting</u> <u>eagerly</u> <u>just</u> <u>as</u> <u>I</u> <u>am</u>, <u>that</u> <u>day</u> <u>in</u> <u>the</u> <u>near</u> <u>future</u> <u>when</u> <u>we'll</u> <u>be</u> <u>together</u> <u>again</u>.

Do you remember that strawberry shortcake you made me last summer Darling, I certainly wish I had a piece of it now.

I've been hearing of different articles being strictly rationed back there, especially coffee. If I was back there now it seems as though your mom and I would have to talk over a pot of coca instead of coffee. Well the rations won't be for long, because I frankly believe the European war will be over for the end of <u>1943</u>. I say a prayer for you Darling and every body back there every night....

It's been so long since I've lain in a real bed and taken all my clothes off to sleep that it's going to feel mighty strange when I do get a real bed to sleep in....

Glad to hear Mike is in a good place and pray he continues to stay there for the duration.

Martha's brother Mike was shipped to the vital Panama Canal days after the Japanese attack on Hawaii in December 1941. Nazi agents in South America and Japanese naval forces planned to attack the Panama Canal and destroy its locks; their efforts never advanced beyond the planning stage. Mike (also called Mickey) had returned from canal defense duty and was stationed in the US. (During World War II, the United States maintained four air forces and two armies in the United States to defend the homeland, its citizens, and industries.)

Darling, when you're mom bakes bread try to learn how to bake it, because I like that home baked bread. Will you do that for me Martha Darling.

Martha Darling, if you receive this letter before Mar. 25, [the day Martha and Borys met] will you play the Blue Danube Waltz on your sisters recording, on Mar. 25th at 6:00 P.M. N. Y. time and no matter where I am or what I'm doing, I'll stop for 5 minutes and think of you playing it or actually think I'm holding you or dancing with you on Mar. 25th... here's a little verse to you from me for Valentines Day.

Although you are so far away
My love is with you on this day

Your heart and soul are only mine

So on this day sweetheart, you are My Valentine

Loving You Always Martha Darling with all my heart and soul.

Loving You Forever Only Yours,

Borys   XXXXX ♥ XXXXX ♥ XXXXX ♥ XXXXX ♥ XXXXX

True to his word, on their anniversary date, Borys lay awake inside his pup tent striking matches to read the time on his wristwatch; then, he began humming "The Blue Danube."

5

March 1943

Vicinity of Constantine, Algeria

Throughout March, Borys received letters from Martha and home, with the oldest dated 16 January 1943 from his parents. It now appeared there was little chance of receiving any more letters from 1942. Additionally, Borys received a package from Martha containing items he had requested, such as soap, lots of candy, ten stamped air mail envelopes, writing paper, plain envelopes, and gum. He immediately used the stationery and air mail envelopes. Martha had enclosed eight three-cent stamps in two separate letters, and her sister Mary sent six three-cent stamps in her own letter. (Air mail was six cents, while regular mail was free.)

Borys's letters included his usual statements asking how Martha's family was in the opening and best wishes and blessings in closing. He informed Martha who he had received letters from and to whom he had written. In March, Borys sent Martha a Soldier's Letter, commonly referred as a "blue envelope" letter due to the blue color of the envelope. These letters must "…refer only to personal or family matters." No officer in his regiment would be able to read the letter; censorship was required from an officer in another outfit.

<u>My Own</u> Dearest Darling Martha,

Am glad to hear you've been receiving most of my mail, but it is very slow getting to me. <u>Darling</u>, please excuse the dirt or finger marks on the paper, because I haven't taken a bath for close to 2 weeks now.

Gee Darling, you make me happy when you said a single bed or none... I'm in an awkward position on my stomach writing this letter. I'm all sun burned now, walking around with my shirt off all during the day... It's awful hot right here now Darling...

In your Jan. 26th letter you say it's only natural for you & I to have a few children, but Darling if you leave matters like that up to me, I won't know when to stop. Please put a <u>limit</u> to me Darling, because you know the kind of a wolf I am <u>with you</u>.

My sister Helen wrote in my moms letter that she can play violin and has already played in some high school auditorium with some other children. She's a smart little girl and catches on to things quick...

Martha Darling, I'll bet you're going to be pretty busy for a while with Marys Baby and you had better get plenty of practice changing diapers Darling, for when that husband (<u>Borys</u>) of yours gets back to you, I know he's going to keep you busy with his little <u>babies</u> that his <u>wife</u> <u>Martha</u> will present him.

<u>Martha</u> <u>Darling</u>, I received your letter yesterday that was dated Feb. 21st telling me of my moms visit to you. As I'm writing this letter to you Dearest, I've just received a letter from home also telling me of my moms visit to you. <u>Martha</u> <u>Darling</u>, my mom tells me she was treated swell and enjoyed her visit very much. That was swell of you Darling to see my mom every day and take her back to the station. Isn't there anything I can give you besides my love for treating my mom so well. She thinks the world of you Darling.

Gee Martha Darling, that's the best news I could ever want to hear, <u>you saying that you love & love me with all your heart</u>. <u>I love you also Martha Darling and will forever love you</u>.

My sister Sue told me of getting another baby around July [Sue already had two girls, Anna and Josie]. <u>Martha Darling</u>, it looks as though everybody is getting a big head start on us, but we'll catch up, won't we Dearest....

Perhaps by now or in a few days Mary will be having her baby. I hope to win the bet and get them 25 real kisses from you Darling. <u>Supposing</u> I lose and she gets a baby girl what will my penalty be for losing the bet? Please don't be to harsh with me if I lose the bet Darling. I'll tell you what Darling, if I lose the bet, I'll only be able <u>to kiss you 24</u> times, okay.

Again I send my loyal, undying, devoted love to you Martha Darling. Martha Darling, God had gifted some men with riches, some with power, <u>but above these things and above everything, he has gifted me with a true love, your love Martha Darling. Our love for each other Darling is priceless. Nothing can harm you Martha Darling, nor any human, for my life will have to be taken before anyone will ever harm you. I love you so much Darling that I'd live through a million hells and then give my life for you if I had to</u>.

As March 1943 closed, the army implemented a new mail security procedure. All Xs representing kisses were now censored from all letters home. During the waning days of the month, the army censor cut off the corner of the last page of Borys's letter where he had written the Xs signifying kisses to Martha. In addition, underlining

words would be prohibited. Borys would inform Martha of the new censorship regu-
lation in a letter he wrote in April 1943.

The final mail call in March brought a letter from Martha written 6 February for
Valentine's Day. Martha's letter started with her usual warm salutation:

My Darling Butch, My Beloved,

I love you.

*I had to start this Valentine's Day letter expressing my innermost
feelings.*

I love you are words I have said to no other man.

*I love you is my most intimate, heartfelt and deepest sentiments
toward you.*

I love you.

*I had to say it again and again; I cannot say it enough. I wish
we were together so I could say, "I love you," as we kissed and
embraced.*

We share this same thought of devotion to one another.

I know this to be true from our moments together and your writings.

*We also share a similar enthusiasm that our first child be a girl
named "Patricia-Ann."*

*Butch, My love. I yearn to be with you so we can dance as we did
on our first date. I continually think of our opening dance at the Prospect Park Picnic House as we waltzed to the tune of the Blue Danube.*

*It was so wonderful to be held in your arms as we glided across
the floor.*

You are my Valentine, Borys. This day and every time we are

together for I love you. Borys, you are my Valentine when we are
apart. I long for us to be together for I do love you.
Thank you for being my Valentine, Borys, my love.

Martha wrote that her mother, father, and sisters, all sent their love. She sent surrogate regards from her brothers since they were all in the service now. Most importantly, all wished Borys a speedy and safe return to the US. She enclosed a very special present, a lock of her hair.

Martha provided news from the home front. She organized a scrap metal drive on her block for the war effort. The neighbors, who shared a common driveway, agreed to donate the six-foot iron gates to the driveway's entrance, which weighed several hundred pounds. The block ended up contributing numerous tons of metal. Martha's father contributed Johnny's old bronze photography award; her father even gave spare brass doorknobs and hinges off doors for scrap. Brass was in high demand since it contained copper and zinc; bronze was comprised of copper and tin.

Copper, precious copper, was needed to make shell casings for artillery, small arms ammunition, and wiring for ships, tanks, airplanes, radar, and other military needs. It was in such short supply that in 1943, the US Treasury stopped making pennies out of copper and, instead, used steel coated with zinc.

In 1944, millions of shell casings were returned to the US, and production of pennies once again used copper, albeit with a composition more similar to the shell casings than earlier bronze pennies.

Copper was in such short supply that the most secret project of the war, the Manhattan Project, which developed the atomic bomb, was forced to use a substitute metal for wiring. They borrowed an electrical conductor better than copper from the US Treasury—silver. After the war, the silver was returned and, years later, the secret revealed.

More good news from the home front: her sister Mary was due to give birth to her first child in early March.

Martha's Valentine's Day letter was Borys's lucky charm; it would see him through the war. He put it in the left breast pocket of his fatigue shirt, near his heart and kept it there throughout the war.

In reply to Martha's Valentine's Day letter, Borys wrote:

March 31,ˢᵗ 1943

No. Africa

9:00 P.M.

My Own Dearest Beloved Martha,

Have received a letter today dated Feb. 6ᵗʰ containing your lock of hair and the 4-3 cent stamps. Gee Martha Darling, it was swell of you to send the lock of hair with the pink ribbon tied around. Pink is for a baby girl, so Darling our first baby will have to be a girl, but if our first baby is a boy, we won't be discouraged, because Darling, there's a saying that quotes as follows—If You Don't Succeed the First time, Try Again.

Gee Darling, the lock of your hair makes me feel as though I were next to you, and will be with me until the day I die. Just as your going to show my lock to our Patrica, I'll show your lock to her and tell our Patrica her mothers lock of hair was an inspiration to me during the war and gave me more courage than anything to get back to her, you Darling.

The heart attached to the letter was sweet of you Darling and your kisses next to it were swell because they were put there with all your heart and Love in it to me. The poem was swell Darling. One part of a line in particular which I'll quote over is the truth Martha Darling. "I Love/Need You." Yes Martha Dearest I love You and I need you, because without you my life would be empty. I love you & love you Martha Darling Beloved Mine.

Darling I'm going to finish this letter later for my little light in my pup tent is blinding me with smoke. I'm now going to sleep on my straw mattress on the ground, and praying God will end this war soon, so I can get back to you Martha Darling, and get married, so that we can have our own little home and family. I love you Martha Dearest and I'll dream of you and think I'm next to you. Good Night Darling.

The Battle of the Atlantic still raged, and news of the catastrophic losses was kept silent, with the press reporting only a fraction of the true figure. Favorite targets along the US coast were oil tankers and ships carrying bauxite from Jamaica for producing aluminum to construct airplanes. As American countermeasures to U-boats became effective along the coast and in the Caribbean, the Nazis shifted their submarine attacks much farther east to the mid–North Atlantic Ocean. They also struck at Allied shipping between South America and Africa.

By the end of 1942, German submarines had sunk over one thousand Allied ships and had lost fewer than ninety U-boats. During the first three weeks of March 1943, the maritime slaughter reached its height, with more than half a million tons of Allied supplies sinking to the Atlantic's depths.

The United States built almost one hundred new shipyards to construct warships and other vessels such as the Liberty ship, a mass-produced cargo carrier capable of transporting extraordinary quantities of military supplies. By 1943, 140 Liberty ships were being built each month, and they were constructed in an average of forty-one days. By the end of 1945, around twenty-seven hundred Liberty ships had been built in American shipyards, which aided in the shipment of nearly 127 million tons of cargo overseas. In 1944 and 1945, over five hundred Victory ships were also built to carry cargo. The major improvement incorporated in Victory ships over Liberty ships was their turbine engines, which increased the maximum speed. Nearly two million shipyard workers, including almost a quarter-million women, built three thousand other ships, including over fifteen hundred naval vessels. The production time also decreased in each class of ship; for example, aircraft carriers were now built in fifteen months, less than half the time it had taken to build a carrier before the war.

6

April 1943

Vicinity of Constantine and Algiers, Algeria

On the Tunisian front, April saw the height of the air-sea and air-air battle to stop the Axis flow of supplies to Africa from France and Italy, including Sicily. In three weeks, 432 Axis aircraft were permanently removed from the skies, with the loss of thirty-five Allied planes. As April 1943 ended, the Allies controlled the skies over North Africa.

Allied mines, ships, and planes sank much of the cargo and fuel destined for the Axis ground forces in Tunisia. With dwindling stocks of munitions and petroleum, German and Italian forces weakened but fought on toward their inevitable end—defeat.

The 62nd AAA Regiment continued its mission of defending B-17 bomber and P-38 fighter airfields. Defensive measures involved training and target practice to hone the accuracy and efficiency of the antiaircraft artillery crews. Additional training required the men to rotate positions on the 90-mm M1A1 gun to get experience on all tasks in case a fellow GI was incapacitated from injury or death. The training resulted in an increase of the rate of cannon fire—now approaching thirty rounds per minute. After repeated firing, all men had a temporary decrease in hearing with ringing in the ears plus "rattling of the bones" due to the concussions from the cannon's firing. Borys had one more unusual concussion-related effect, which he explained to Martha:

My Own Dearly Beloved Martha,

Darling, the watch my pop gave me is broken for good... Do you remember the watch used to keep time for our meeting every night...

After the target practice, Borys looked at the wristwatch his father had given him. His heart sank to the pit of his stomach as he realized the watch crystal and hands had fallen off again during firing. Borys ran to the gun position and searched around; first, he found the crystal broken, then the minute hand, followed by the hour hand—all were damaged.

Have received a letter from you Darling, dated Feb. 24th, telling me of you & Blondie [the nickname for Martha's sister Ann] seeing my mom off at the bus terminal. It was swell of you Martha Darling to see my mom every day and help her to get back. You're a Darling, and regardless what you say Martha Darling, I can honestly say that I'm a lucky man to have a girl as sweet as you to love and be my wife. Only one man in a thousand can get a girl like you Darling, and I'm lucky to have you and your love.

Don't bawl me out Darling, but you are a Dear and I place you above my own life Darling. I realize you can't send packages Darling, so I'll just have to do with out them, and please don't worry over it Darling....

So people can't buy much liquor now back there. I guess it won't hurt them to drink more water....

I was certainly glad to hear that Mary & Jims son was healthy, and send my sincerest congratulations to the both of them. I'll bet it was quite an occasion at your home.

Regardless if I lost the bet with you Darling, [twenty-five kisses for a baby boy] it wouldn't have made any difference for I know you would have given me your love and kisses....

I won the bet alright Martha Darling, and only wish I was with you to collect them precious kisses. Darling, I'll tell you what to do of them kisses, keep them warm in your heart and when I get back to you, well Darling, you'll give them to me all at once and perhaps I may take a few extra as interest....

Martha Darling, the verse in the Easter Card is swell. I've re-read it a few times and I can only say, I Love You Martha Darling. You say you don't care for apartments to live in, well Darling frankly, I don't care for them either. You ask my opinion of the kind of a home I'd like, well Martha Darling, my idea of a home is the same as yours.

Martha Darling, as far as picking our home, it'll be all up to you Darling, for as myself I just want to make you happy Darling, and you as my wife Martha Darling, I'll always be happy to love you and have your love. As for our furniture for our home Darling, I'm going to give you the job of picking it all, for it's only right to have you Darling to pick our home and furniture. You see Martha Darling, with you happy, I'll also be happy. There is only one thing I'll pick Darling, our single bed.

Martha Darling, I don't know much of cost of furniture so you can buy it wherever you please to buy it Darling. Martha Darling, will you please try to figure out roughly the cost of everything. By that I mean our wedding in church, our wedding party, the whole cost of our wedding in General, our furniture, and our honeymoon. Please give me a general idea Darling, just so you and I will know. Please figure everything as best as possible Darling. I know it'll be over a thousand dollars, so Martha Darling, I'm just going to get a job as soon as possible after I'm discharged from the army.

Tell your mom, I'll always have a pot of coffee on the stove for her and I everyday she comes to see us, ...

Thanks ever so much Darling for playing the Anniversary Waltz on our Anniversary, and I pray our next anniversary, we'll be together, and we'll dance to it for a whole half hour....

Martha Darling, due to new censorship regulations, we're not permitted to underline any words, or put kisses in the form of crosses in any of our letters, so it doesn't matter Darling for you know I love you and forever will love you...

The space in the left corner is left to represent my kisses for you Martha Darling.

Loving You Always Forever,
Borys

Upon receipt of Martha's Easter Card and one from her parents, Borys wrote, "I pray we can all be together for next Easter, in your home and at the table." He also wished Martha and her family a Happy Easter, and sent her letters and V-mail to Mary, Johnny, home, and his siblings, Sue and Teddy.

Stateside, the start of the baseball season in April rekindled the rivalry between the New York Yankees and the Boston Red Sox. Being a native New Yorker, Martha was a Yankees fan, while Borys, from Massachusetts, was a Red Sox fan. The October 1943 World Series would define the year's best baseball team. The lucrative sum of twenty-five kisses going to the winner was up for grabs: if the Yankees won the World Series, Martha would collect, but if the Red Sox won, Borys would recover his 1942 bet.

Good Friday, 23 April 1943, was the beginning of the end for the Axis armies in Tunisia. Now cornered in northeast Tunisia with their backs to the sea, the Allies intended to have three hundred thousand American, British, and French troops strike at the Axis forces along the length of a 140-mile arc. They would have about fourteen hundred tanks and an equal number of artillery pieces for support.

The Americans would attack Bizerte and the British would attack Tunis, the capital of Tunisia. In less than three weeks, the Allies would have their final victory in North Africa.

Meanwhile, in Algeria, the 62nd AAA Regiment prepared to shift its location. At 0800 hours on 29 April 1943, movement began to Algiers by motor transportation. When the convoy arrived the following afternoon, positions were taken around Algiers for the defense of the city and port, including the difficult and tedious task of digging the guns in.

April saw a turnaround in the Battle of the Atlantic with better and more convoy escorts, and improved training and tactics. In addition to planes from the escort carriers, the Allies used long-range bombers to close the mid-Atlantic air gap in their hunt for German submarines.

U-boats were now sailing at risk on the ocean's surface, with enhanced Allied radar detecting and aiding in sinking them. Forced underwater, the U-boats were slower and lacked endurance. May 1943 would be the decisive month in the Battle of the Atlantic.

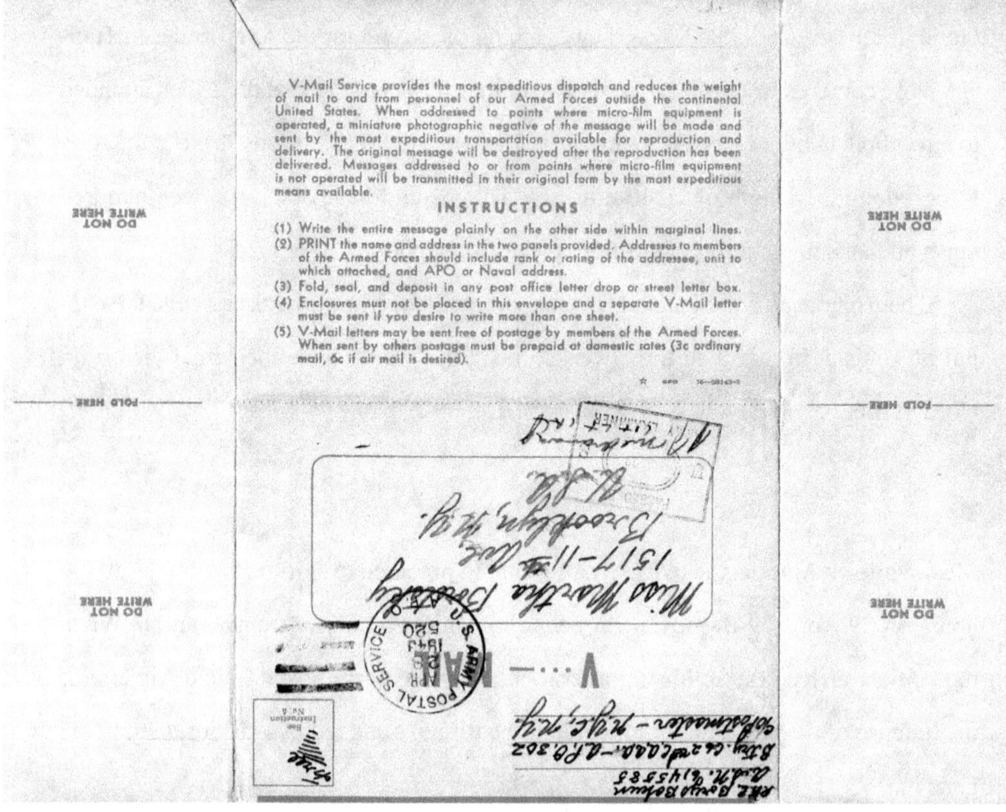

V-Mail Service provides the most expeditious dispatch and reduces the weight of mail to and from personnel of our Armed Forces outside the continental United States. When addressed to points where micro-film equipment is operated, a miniature photographic negative of the message will be made and sent by the most expeditious transportation available for reproduction and delivery. The original message will be destroyed after the reproduction has been delivered. Messages addressed to or from points where micro-film equipment is not operated will be transmitted in their original form by the most expeditious means available.

INSTRUCTIONS

(1) Write the entire message plainly on the other side within marginal lines.
(2) PRINT the name and address in the two panels provided. Addresses to members of the Armed Forces should include rank or rating of the addressee, unit to which attached, and APO or Naval address.
(3) Fold, seal, and deposit in any post office letter drop or street letter box.
(4) Enclosures must not be placed in this envelope and a separate V-Mail letter must be sent if you desire to write more than one sheet.
(5) V-Mail letters may be sent free of postage by members of the Armed Forces. When sent by others postage must be prepaid at domestic rates (3c ordinary mail, 6c if air mail is desired).

V-mail (Victory mail) letter written by Borys on 27 April 1943. The letter contains instructions for use and directions on where to fold it. Notice the censor's stamp and signature on both the outside and the inside (below) of the letter.

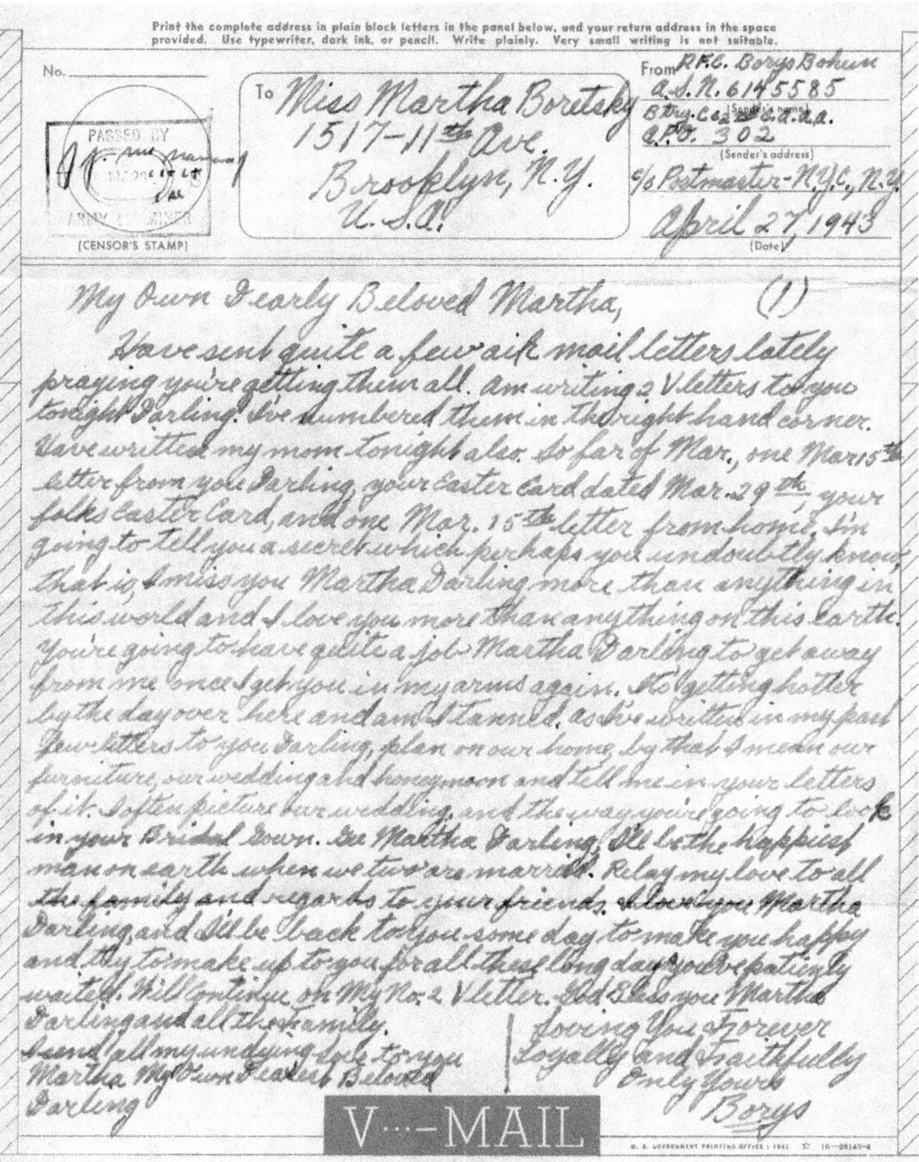
Print the complete address in plain block letters in the panel below, and your return address in the space provided. Use typewriter, dark ink, or pencil. Write plainly. Very small writing is not suitable.
No.
PASSED BY
ARMY EXAMINER
(CENSOR'S STAMP)
To Miss Martha Boretsky
1517-11th Ave.
Brooklyn, N.Y.
U.S.A!
From Pfc. Borys Bohun
A.S.N. 6145585
Btry. Co. Ea.a.a.
A.P.O. 302
(Sender's address)
c/o Postmaster-N.Y.C., N.Y.
April 27 1943
(Date)
My Own Dearly Beloved Martha,   (1)
Have sent quite a few air mail letters lately praying you're getting them all. Am writing 2 V letters to you tonight Darling. I've numbered them in the right hand corner. Have written my mom tonight also. So far of Mar., one Mar.15th letter from you Darling, your Easter card dated Mar. 29th, your folks Easter card, and one Mar. 15th letter from home. I'm going to tell you a secret which perhaps you undoubtly know, that is, I miss you Martha Darling more than anything in this world and I love you more than anything on this Earth. You're going to have quite a job Martha Darling to get away from me once I get you in my arms again. It's getting hotter by the day over here and am I tanned, as I've written in my past few letters to you Darling, plan on our home, by that I mean our furniture, our wedding and honeymoon and tell me in your letters of it. Soften picture our wedding, and the way you're going to look in your Bridal Gown. Oh Martha Darling, I'll be the happiest man on earth when we two are married. Relay my love to all the family and regards to your friends. I love you Martha Darling, and I'll be back to you some day to make you happy and try to make up to you for all these long days you'll patiently wait. Will continue on my No. 2 V letter. God Bless you Martha Darling and all the family.
I send all my undying love to you Martha My Own Dearest Beloved Darling
Loving You Forever Loyally and Faithfully Only Yours Borys
V----MAIL
U. S. GOVERNMENT PRINTING OFFICE : 1943

7

May 1943

Algiers, Algeria

With ever-increasing air, sea, and land forces in North Africa, the Allies sank hundreds of Axis ships in the Mediterranean Sea, amounting to more than half a million tons of military cargo from the inception of the campaign to its end in May 1943. Their strategy paid off, as the lack of fuel, munitions, food, and other supplies further isolated German and Italian forces in North Africa to one diminishing corner of Tunisia.

The stress of war—with its death and destruction—demonstrated to men how vulnerable they were. It began taking its toll on Borys, as revealed in his 6 May 1943 letter to Martha:

My Own Dearly Beloved Martha,

Martha Darling, here's the man that loves you very much writing to you again, letting you know he loves you very much....Got 2 letters from My brother Ted, one dated Mar. 29th and Apr. 15th, letting me know of his recent illness. Perhaps or most likely by now he's in the army, which I think is a damned Shame. If my folks have written you,

I believe they told you of the heart attack he got and injuring his head while falling, putting him unconscious for 3 days and putting him close to death. It's too bad and I felt bad of the incident and thank God he recovered for the sake of his wife & child.

Because of Teddy's heart attack and related injury, the US Army would not accept him for service. Instead, he became a merchant marine and served on merchant ships, sailing in convoys with ships targeted and sunk by U-boats. Teddy's service included the extremely dangerous Soviet ports of Murmansk and Archangel. Merchant ships and their escorts were not only subject to attacks from U-boats on the northern route but also from surface German warships and aircraft from captured Norwegian airfields.

Most likely you know of my brother Andrew enlisting in the Navy. He's a good kid & will make out good in his service in the Navy. I pray nothing ever happens to him for he's only a kid & hasn't seen life yet. The pen ran dry so I borrowed ink which is different color. I hope I get your mail soon for it's quite some time I heard from you Martha Darling, you know I love you very much & I know you're true to me & love me.

I'm going to ask something of you Martha Darling, that isn't a pleasant subject to talk of, but it deals with reality. Remember Martha Darling, I love you with all my heart and soul and if God spares my life, I'll return to you to live life as we planned, to get married, have our own home, and undoubtedly our Patrica Ann & family, and have our love & happiness together just as we've known & know we've had when we were together. I'm asking this of you Martha

Darling, and I know you love me and will do it, please Darling.

If anything ever happens that I can't prevent, that is if I never am able to return to you, please Martha Darling, don't ruin your life because of it. You're young Martha Darling, and very pretty, and many a man would give anything to have you as his wife.

I feel that someday I'll come back to you Martha Darling, but just in case it's the opposite, I'd want you to keep your chin up and do your best to forget. If anything ever happens to me, keep what little money we're saving for yourself. It's an unpleasant subject to talk of Martha Darling, but just in case anything happened please Martha Darling, it may be hard, but I know you'll do what I've asked.

Knowing you as I do Martha Darling, I'll bet when I get back to you, you'll have everything planned well for our marriage & home. You're a Darling Martha & I love you.

Get plenty of practice on changing diapers Martha Darling, for you'll have quite a job changing Patrica Anns & undoubtedly one or two or 5 or 6 of our own children.

All My Undying Love, Loving You Forever, Only Yours,
Borys

As May progressed, Borys received letters from their two families. New postal regulations limited the size of overseas packages to eight ounces for a time. He replied to correspondence from his parents and siblings, and he wrote to Martha's parents and her siblings.

My Own Dearly Beloved Martha,

...Martha Darling, I wish I could get a small full picture of yourself. If you get a chance Darling, try to get one made. Martha Darling, I'm going to give you heck if you keep teasing me in my dreams. I've got a lot to tell you Darling of different dreams I've had of you. I'll tell you when we're together again.... Boy am I getting strong, but when you get me in your arms Darling, I'll bet you'll know how to control me, but be careful Martha Darling, because I'll try my best to try to find ways to get extra kisses from you....

... As far as the number of children we'll have Darling, after we're ahead, we'll let nature take it's course. Martha Darling if we let nature take its course, my God, we'll have an army. You'll have to put a limit on me Darling, for I'll never know when to stop, Mm, Mm....Glad to hear you got a stack of my letters all at once. Will try to get some pictures of myself soon and send to you Darling. Dearest the one package I got from you couldn't have been insured for I didn't have to sign for it, but the others you sent that were insured I never got and are surely lost by now.

Have received Marys letter... Mary tells me Jim may be drafted soon. Sorry to hear it. Was glad to hear the baby was getting along well.... How is our Opera Star Lizzie?

Darling, have just received your letter today containing your picture. The letter was dated May 9th. Gee honey, was I glad to get one of your latest letters, for I know you're well and everything is alright. There is a lot of your back mail I haven't received yet but I don't mind so much, even though I'd like to get them. I don't mind it so much for when I get a letter from you Darling only taking 14 days it makes happy knowing it was just written recently.

Why Martha Dearest you look swell & beautiful in your picture, and sweet. Gee Darling, I could squeeze you out of that picture and just love you & kiss you. Darling, you're just adorable & I could worship you of which I do. I don't know how I was ever so lucky to meet you, and have your love, and have you as my own.... Thanks a lot Dearest for sending me Andy's address, for I didn't as yet receive it from my folks.... I'll write Andrew sometimes today or tomorrow.

There isn't much doubt that the packages are lost that you've sent quite a while back & eventually when they check up, you'll be entitled to get the money back for the cost of everything, for the packages were insured. It may take quite some time but eventually you can get the claims on them. I'll let you know Darling when I get Mary's 8 oz. & your package.

It's swell of you Dearest to light a candle for me every Sunday. I say a prayer for you Martha Darling & everyone back there every night.

I Love You Martha Darling, Always Forever Yours.

All My Undying Love Loving You Forever Only Yours,

Borys

Martha sent a single picture of herself as Borys requested.

On 6 May, the Allies initiated their plan for an American assault on the port city of
Bizerte, with the British attacking the capital city of Tunis. After an intense artillery
pounding and a follow-up concentrated aerial bombing, Axis defenses crumbled. Both
cities fell the following day; Bizerte was destroyed, while Tunis was mainly intact
except for the port area.

On 12 May 1943, the air raid alert in Algiers sounded at 2045 hours. Determined
to stop the destruction in Algiers by seven Nazi bombers, the antiaircraft artillerymen

fired an intense volley of flak, destroying the aircraft bombing plans along with most of the planes. The all-clear sounded at 2130 hours. Antiaircraft defenses were credited with five planes and the British Royal Air Force (RAF) with two planes; the entire raiding formation was annihilated! During the past six months, the cannoneers had successfully learned the skills the Axis powers had developed more than three years before—that is, how to fight a war. As a result of this attack, two 62nd AAA Regiment GIs received Purple Hearts for shrapnel wounds sustained in the attack.

On 13 May 1943, an air raid alert in Algiers sounded at 2135 hours. The estimated size of the raid was twenty-five to thirty planes. Antiaircraft defenses were credited with destroying five "certain" and two "probable" planes through radar-controlled firing. Claims for the British-made Beaufighter airplanes were not determined but believed to be similar.

The Axis forces in Africa realized the futility of their struggle and surrendered in Tunisia on 13 May 1943. The Allies defeated the best the Third Reich and Italian Fascists threw at them and took over two hundred thousand prisoners.

On 27 May 1943, three officers and two warrant officers were given a five-day course in loading matériel aboard landing craft. This was in preparation for the next invasion, which was of an unknown destination.

The victory in North Africa and the arrival of tens of thousands of fresh troops brought hope of returning home. However, this expectation was soon shattered since they were combat experienced and earmarked for the invasion of Europe. The 62nd AAA Regiment GIs were told they would not go home until the "mission of defeating the enemy is accomplished." This news dashed Borys's hopes of returning to Martha for her eighteenth birthday, but he still optimistically believed the war would end by Christmas 1943 with an Allied victory.

The demand for a large military, along with the tremendous industrial output, led to a severe labor shortage filled by women, blacks, and agricultural workers.

Almost nineteen million women worked for pay during the war. Women not only contributed to the war effort in manufacturing but, like Martha, millions volunteered to do war-related tasks, such as attending reception centers and entertaining troops, serving as Office of Price Administration (OPA) price monitors, or helping pack Red Cross surgical dressings.

Around 350,000 women voluntarily enlisted in the armed services, including:

- Army WACs (Women's Army Corps)
- Navy WAVES (Women Accepted for Voluntary Emergency Service)
- Air Corps WASPS (Women's Auxiliary Service Pilots)
- Coast Guard SPARS (from coast guard Latin motto *Semper Paratus*)
- Marine women volunteers (no nickname)
- Civilian female munitions WOWs (Women Ordnance Workers)

To protect the convoys, newly constructed escort carriers or small aircraft carriers patrolled with convoys. Ships and aircraft were equipped with newly-improved radar. Planes patrolled forward and on both flanks of convoys rather than above them to combat German wolf packs before they could attack the convoy.

With Allied advances in technology, such as new homing torpedoes, better intelligence and tactics, and the mass production of cargo carriers, escort ships, and planes, the tide of battle in the Atlantic began to turn during the second quarter of 1943.

In May, over forty U-boats were sent to the ocean's depths, and wolf packs were recalled. Individual U-boats still menacingly prowled the perilous ocean waters seeking prey, only for many to become fatalities.

It was not until September 1943 that the U-boat reappeared in greater numbers in the Atlantic. During the remainder of 1943, German submarines sank sixty-seven Allied ships but lost almost an equal number of U-boats. There was no doubt on either side of the conflict that the Allies had won the Battle of the Atlantic. However, U-boats would continue to menace Allied shipping until the war's end—at great peril to the submarines and their crew.

American industrial might was spiking. US auto manufacturers, the largest in the world, had ceased production to make mobile weapons, such as tanks, self-propelled artillery, and aircraft.

8

JUNE 1943

Algiers, Algeria, and Bizerte, Tunisia

Preparation for the impending invasion of a still-unknown destination ramped up in early June. On the first, two officers and four enlisted men were sent to the Fifth Army Invasion Training Center for a four-day course in the waterproofing of motor vehicles. The next day, a captain and six enlisted men were sent to the Fifth Army Invasion Training Center for a four-day course in waterproofing of matériel as a follow-up to the five-day course in loading matériel aboard landing crafts on 27 May.

On the fourth of June, a captain and three enlisted men started a ten-day British aircraft recognition course. That day, the air raid alert sounded at 2215 hours, and the 62nd AAA went into action with the flash and roar of cannons. The Third Battalion's searchlights illuminated five German planes, and radar control aided in the destruction of one Nazi raider. Multiple bombs straddled one battery's position and two searchlight positions; a radar antenna suffered damage. The all-clear sounded at 2250 hours.

On 17 June, the 62nd Regiment began movement to Bizerte, Tunisia, by motor transportation. Upon the convoy's arrival on 20 June at 1430 hours, the batteries were assigned to protect troop concentrations of an infantry division in the staging area for the impending invasion.

June brought few letters to Borys from Martha and her family and, of course, his family. On the bright side, he received two eight-ounce packages—one from Martha and the other from her sister, Mary. Borys wrote Martha:

My Own Dearly Beloved Martha,

Martha Dearest, it'll be over 10 months we've been apart after you've received this letter. It's been 10 months of hell being away from you Darling, but even if it takes over another year Dearest apart from you or even a life time, it would mean more to me just to be with you again and feel your hair, kiss you & look into your eyes, than anything I've ever wanted on this earth. I hope & pray that I can make you as happy as the happiness you've given to me when I get back to you Darling.

It wasn't for long we were together, but long enough to find out that I found a girl I've always longed for & love. My only regret is that I had to leave you Darling & know that the length of time being away from you, would leave you in worry & loneliness. I guess there isn't much I could do to prevent this, just as your brothers & thousands of others are being taken away from their loved ones, praying daily with the hopes of returning back to the ones they possess so Dearly. We all have hopes that God will return us safely, but only he knows what is in store for us. I've never felt so confident that I am coming back to you Darling and all I ask of you Dearest is not to worry....

Martha Darling, I don't have to tell you I love you, for you know it & I'll forever love you. It's something that's branded in my heart

& can only burn out when I cease to live. I've nothing in the way of riches to offer you, nothing but my love for you, a home which won't be a mansion, but I can give you my love which you already have, a small home of our own & above all, our own little family and a few arguments to make us happy....

...Mail to me has been slow for the past few months. A lot of mail must be lost. Told you in my last letter to you Darling, of getting yours & Marys 8 oz. packages, also signed a postal claim slip for the packages you & your mom sent a long while back, [The last months of 1942.] and I never received.

It was swell of you Darling to have had a mass for your brothers & I. As sure as your praying for me Martha Darling, I feel and know the day can't be to far away when I'll be in your arms again Darling. Every time I look at your pictures, I think of the times I held you & kissed you, & I keep longing & longing to hold you again....

I just can't wait for the day you & I go to pick our furniture for our home & the day we go to church & be united as one. It'll be a picture that will always live in my mind to see you in your wedding gown & you holding my arm coming from the alter....

...Ted tells me he was rejected from the army due to his recent illness... Perhaps my sister Helen may go to N.Y. with mom, if so ask her if she can play the Anniversary Waltz on the violin. Ted tells me my brother Steve has been home for quite some time, & he seems a lot better. [Steve was discharged from the Marine Corps due to a heart condition.] He often asks about me, so Teddy tells me....

As you know the war is over in Africa, but while this war was still on, I got discouraged a few times and requested a transfer even to front line action, but couldn't get it. Its going on 5 yrs. that I've served in our army and am only a P.F.C. & is discouraging. I know sincerely if I could have been in some other outfit, I could have easily attained a sergeantcy.

Borys was discharged as a sergeant after three years of army service in October 1941; he had reenlisted after the Japanese attack on the United States with the rank of private.

The reason I wanted to get out and better my grade is so I could send you more... Perhaps today I'm better off, for I'm feeling fine & am in one piece....

...On this 24ᵗʰ day of June years back a sweet girl was born, my future wife, you Martha Darling. My Love & best wishes to you Darling on this day, knowing I'll be with you on your next birthday & even before. I expect & look forward to more than anything on this earth to have you as my wife Martha Darling before the end of 1944.

I can only say when the day of our marriage, my life will just begin & I know when that day does come, you're going to be just as happy as I will be....

Sue will be getting her baby soon, and looks like everyone is getting babies, so Martha Darling have no fear, for this wolf that loves you so much is going to catch up to them all when we get married....

As I've asked before Darling, I'd like if you'd try to figure & let me know about the approximate amount for our wedding, honeymoon & our home. Here's my idea Darling. I can't say for sure, but approximately – our wedding about $250 – our honeymoon – about

$250 – our home – bedroom set $200 – parlor set $200 – kitchen set about $150 – frigidaire $100 – odds & ends for our home around $100 – a radio $100. Please let me know about how you figure it Darling, for you could have a better idea than me....

I Love & Adore you Martha My Own Dearly Beloved Darling. God Bless your sweet little heart, your heart that I love so Dearly. God Bless All the family. All My Undying Love.

Loving You Forever Martha My Beloved, Only Yours,
Borys

9

JULY 1943

Bizerte, Tunisia

The 62nd Coast Artillery Antiaircraft Regiment convoy arrived at its bivouac east of Ferryville, Tunisia, on 20 June 1943. All batteries had positions on the east shore of Lake Bizerte, and their mission was to protect troop concentrations in the staging area. The regiment's sixteen 90-mm guns, along with its .50s and 40-mms, were the last defensive mechanisms protecting the thousands of infantry troops. The cannoneers knew that once Axis planes got through the fighter screen, only antiaircraft outfits would stand in defense of the GIs.

At 0400 hours on 6 July 1943, air raid alerts sounded. All defensive guns were immediately prepared for action. Gun crews waited for instructions on the direction and height of enemy aircraft and orders to fire. Suddenly, both were relayed.

The deafening thunder of cannon fire roared. The Long Toms sent merciless torrents of molten steel to detonate and obliterate their foe.

Changes in distance and height were relayed, and firing resumed; guns were reloaded within seconds, and firing continued over and over.

The radar tracking unceasingly sent information to controls on the guns' mounts, which continued to make adjustments.

Borys and the rest of the crew were unrelenting in their bombardment of the enemy aircraft. The distance kept decreasing as the invaders closed in for the kill.

Volley upon volley exploded in the raiders' flight path, with flak from the ack-ack guns destroying planes and their deadly cargo in midair.

With an increase in distance, the gun crew knew the Axis attackers were beaten and in retreat. Victory was theirs. Yet they fired and loaded and fired again at a rate of about thirty rounds per minute, determined to destroy every plane that dared threaten their brethren.

Once the cease-fire order was received, the squad knew the night fighters would pick up where they had left off; they did. Of the twenty or more enemy aircraft, antiaircraft artillery crews knocked five from the sky. Fighters were believed to have destroyed an equal number, and both groups of defenders were responsible for damaging multiple enemy aircraft. One defender, an enlisted man, received a shrapnel wound.

The all-clear sounded at 0500 hours.

Later that morning, as daylight shined brightly, Borys wrote:

My Own Dearly Beloved Martha,

...Got a letter yesterday from my mom dated June 9th. Very shortly she'll be going to N.Y., & she says she will take some pictures with you. Please send a couple when they're developed, okay Darling.

Martha Darling, I have some surprising news for you. Your brother Johnny was here last Sun. and finally found me. He's looking good. We couldn't go no where because we couldn't get passes for quite some time now. He got to my place Sun. afternoon & stood overnight with me & left Monday morning. I was surprised & glad to see him. He slept in my little pup tent next to me & we talked until after 2 o'clock in the morning before falling asleep. I had some coffee & we made some & had quite a discussion. Gee Darling, it was good to talk to someone so close to you. Took a few pictures together & he'll send them when they're ready. I believe he may try to see Augie very shortly.

I told Johnny you & I will live in B'klyn after we're married.... We talked until the candle burned down to the dry grass in the tent & the grass start burning. I was sorry to see him leave in the morning & perhaps we'll see each other again, but this time I hope it's in B'klyn.

Also heard from Andy [Borys's brother] & he was still in Newport, R.I. at the time.... I'll bet Andy feels pretty good in a sailors uniform....

When Johnny & I were having coffee, I was thinking you're mom would have liked to been with us, for I'm not patting myself on the back, but I'll bet your mom would have enjoyed this coffee because I'm pretty good at making coffee now.

The heat is terrific here now & usually hits 120 degrees in the day time. Sue ought to be getting her baby boy soon, & my mom will most likely be there. Marys baby will be crawling soon & I hope I'm back before he starts walking. Are Jim or Pete in the army?

Jimmy, the husband of Martha's oldest sister, Mary, enlisted in the navy. The second-oldest girl, Ann, was more fortunate, since her husband, Pete, was a longshoreman and had received an occupational deferment from the draft. Pete worked ten, twelve, and more hours a day, seven days a week, to meet the demand of loading ships going overseas.

My brother Alek tells me he'll be getting quite a few vegetables out of his Victory garden.

Martha Darling, it's almost a year we've been apart, & my Love for you Darling is as great as the night I left you. Martha Beloved, when I get you in my arms again, I won't know when to stop loving & kissing you....

Gee Darling, it's all I think of is you, our marriage & home. With you to work for Beloved, it won't take me long to save enough for our marriage after I'm out the army. I feel happy Darling everytime I think of you as my wife, going to carry & give birth to our baby of your blood & my blood.

Photo of Borys (l.) and Johnny (r.) taken in Bizerte, Tunisia.

Borys closed the letter with his regards to Martha's family and his love to her. It was ironic that her brother, Johnny, had stayed with Borys on Independence Day. Americans viewed WWII as a fight to maintain that independence. From the one little seed of freedom planted by their founding fathers on 4 July 1776, an entire forest had grown. Americans had exported and planted seedlings of liberty in North Africa and planned to do the same in Europe.

The question was: Where?

The answer came on 10 July 1943, with Operation Husky, the invasion of Sicily.

PART TWO:

ITALY

10

JULY 1943

Port of Licata, Porto Empedocle, and Palermo, Sicily

Sicily's southern portion was invaded through amphibious landings backed up by a large naval support, including two aircraft carriers. Allied air forces commanded air supremacy over Sicily, and their navies destroyed Axis coastal batteries as men and machines landed in southern Sicily on 10 July and moved inland. The American Seventh Army stormed up the west coast to capture Palermo and then across the northern part of the island to Messina. The Canadians fought north through Sicily's center and met the Americans. In addition, the British Eighth Army battled their way up the east coast, joining their allies in Messina. Meticulous planning by the Allies ensured success, as over one hundred thousand Axis troops were forced to evacuate to Italy within a month, and most of the remaining troops capitulated. There were still diehard holdouts in Sicily for another week, however.

Allied victory in Sicily resulted in the collapse of the Fascist government led by dictator Benito Mussolini on 25 July. King Victor Emmanuel III of Italy had Mussolini imprisoned. The Fascist marshal Pietro Badoglio was chosen as his replacement. The new Italian government under Badoglio surrendered about six weeks later, on 8 September.

The Germans, feeling they had lost an ally, sent sixteen divisions to occupy Italy. Germany's leader, Reich Chancellor "Führer" Adolf Hitler ordered the Italian army disarmed and sent six hundred thousand Italian soldiers to German slave labor camps.

As the time neared to turn the calendar page to August 1943, Borys wrote Martha:

My Own Dearly Beloved Martha,

It's been some time since I have had a chance or time to write to anyone. This is my first opportunity so I'm writing to you Dearest. I'm now out of No. Africa, and am some where in Sicily, so you now know why I haven't been able to write....

I was dreaming of you last night Darling, & I'm awful lonesome for you & hope & know this war can't last to much longer so I can hold you again.

It's 11 months today since we parted and it seems like a long while. Please Martha Darling don't worry, for you're the only girl I ever loved & could ever love. Your everything to me Beloved & without you Darling in the future, my life would be empty. I've everything to look forward to, to get back to you beloved, to marry you & to have our own home & family. There is nothing more I want in life, only you as my wife Martha Darling....

Borys stopped writing the letter, reached into his shirt pocket, and pulled out Martha's Valentine's Day letter. He smiled, looked it over, folded the pages, and returned it to its proper place near his heart. He continued writing:

... I got a second surprise since being overseas. Your brother Augie dropped in to see me that same evening with a friend of his from Texas. Just before he visited me he met Johnny who is also in Sicily.

Augie is looking good & he told me Johnny is getting along fine. He only stood a few hours & had to go back to his camp. I am letting you know this because he may be busy for a few days before writing home.

I hope mail starts to get here very soon for I haven't heard from anyone for quite some time.

All My Undying Love, Loving You Forever Martha My Beloved,

Only Yours,

Borys

The 62nd AAA Regiment had sailed from Bizerte, Tunisia, on 18 July 1943 and landed at Licata, Sicily, the following day. The previous two months of preparation and training contributed to smooth sailing. The regiment disembarked from their LSTs, the abbreviation for Landing Ship, Tank. The LST was built so that it could land virtually anywhere. The bow doors open, and troops and matériel could move out circumventing any obstruction to their mission.

With the M1A1 90-mm guns in tow by the six-ton 6x6 Prime Mover trucks, the regiment moved to Porto Empedocle, a few miles south of Agrigento, Sicily. They stayed there from 19–24 July to provide gun defense for the port before leaving by motor transportation.

The truck convoy traveled almost a hundred miles to Palermo, arriving after midnight on the morning of 25 July 1943, three days after the city's capture by American forces. The convoy suffered no incidents during its travel other than damage to several of its trucks due to difficult navigation on the narrow Sicilian roads at night.

The 62nd Coast Artillery Antiaircraft Regiment's mission was to defend the port and airfield, with the guns and automatic weapons taking positions in the Palermo vicinity. Digging in the guns was made easy for the cannoneers since a number of Italian POWs volunteered in exchange for food and a guarantee *not* to be put in the same stockade as the Germans.

Martha had sent Borys an article from the *New York Sunday News* dated 25 July 1943, and she said the same skirmish, involving her brother Johnny, had been described on radio station WMCA that night. The report described how days earlier, Johnny's armored division had been delayed a few miles outside Palermo, Italy, by an Italian 90-mm artillery piece that had destroyed an American scout half-track armed only with a heavy machine gun.

The article stated the gun was "…on a bend in the road through a rugged gorge bordered by high rocky cliffs." Fortunately, the first shell missed, but the American half-track crew, including Johnny, was forced to abandon their vehicle. "The second shell struck it squarely and reduced it to a mass of wreckage." The crew noted the position of the enemy gun by that first flash and "…pointed out the site of the gun and a 75-mm self-propelled assault gun was rushed up." That started a brief duel that doomed the Italian field gun. When the guys reached the enemy gun, they found a dead Italian lieutenant and a private. Johnny's CO assigned him to go through the lieutenant's personal effects, and he found a letter the man had just finished writing to his family. The radio and newspaper stories said Johnny took the letter along to post with the Italian authorities in Palermo after writing an epitaph on the envelope: "Died at his gun."

11

AUGUST 1943

Palermo, Sicily

At 0415 hours on 1 August 1943, air raid alerts sounded in Palermo, Sicily. A dozen or so Nazi bombers were picked up by radar. By this time in the war, Borys and his fellow antiaircraft artillery crewmen had developed an instinctive reaction to the threat posed by enemy aircraft: the entire team manned harbor battle stations within an instant.

The deafening thunder of cannon fire roared, and muzzle flashes lit the darkness. The cannons sent merciless torrents of molten steel to detonate and obliterate their foe. Volley upon volley exploded in the raiders' flight path, with flak destroying planes and their deadly cargo in midair; still, the Nazi menace drove forward.

An Axis pathfinder plane initiated the bombing attack by dropping flares at both extremities of the harbor to light up the target area. With its silhouette exposed to the attackers, an ammunition ship was struck and violently detonated, destroying everything within the vicinity, including the crew of another battery. Monolithic chunks of concrete, splintered lumber, and searing steel shrapnel pummeled the gun's position. Adding to the catastrophe, an oil dump on the dock ignited with volcanic fury, illuminating the entire port and making two more ships easy prey for the bombers. They, too, were destroyed.

Explosions now straddled the artillerymen's defensive revetments as shrapnel tore through the air threatening life and limb. The GIs dove for protective cover. Suddenly, Borys heard the unmistakable high-pitched whistle of falling bombs directly overhead.

Borys felt one bomb's impact as he lay prone with his hands covering the helmet. Within two seconds of the detonation, a sandbag blown skyward nearly stuck his right side. Most of the protective revetment was destroyed, but its defense saved Borys and the other cannoneers from harm. With the raiders now in retreat, the artillerymen were back at their guns and continued to barrage the sky to pay back the enemy for the damage inflicted, that is, until ceasefire orders were given. Soon afterward, the all-clear sounded.

Stimulated by excess adrenaline, no one slept; they all waited for the grim news. Five enlisted men were killed and thirteen wounded. GIs paid their deepest reverence to the fallen heroes.

The 62nd AAA Regiment was credited with destroying two enemy aircraft (about 17 percent of its force) in the 1 August raid; one crashed into the side of Monte Pellegrino and the other into the sea.

On 2 August, Purple Hearts were awarded to the thirteen enlisted men wounded the previous day.

At 0405 hours on 4 August, the air raid alert sounded in Palermo. Roughly thirty-five German and Italian bombers took part in a raid. The flares were dropped inaccurately and thus did not light the port. The bombs that fell caused minimal damage, including slightly wounding one GI who was awarded the Purple Heart.

Borys was relieved when the artillerymen learned no one was killed during this attack. The antiaircraft fire was highly effective; five aircraft and two probable ones were seen crashing in flames, amounting to around 20 percent of the enemy planes.

Not giving up so easily, the Germans and Italians returned on 6 August 1943, and the air raid alert sounded at 0425 hours. One plane dropped flares to light the port, but the other raider aircraft were driven off. The enemy formation was dispersed when attacked by Allied planes and forced to drop their bombs in the sea.

There was no damage to the port, and the all-clear sounded at 0519 hours. The following two weeks saw relief from bombings for the 62nd AAA Regiment.

With a welcome break in bombing raids, Borys wrote Martha:

My Dearly Beloved Martha,

... I've sent a bunch of pictures to you Darling that Johnny took of Augie [George], himself & two other fellows here in Sicily. I'll explain of it as I already let you know in a small message I put in the package of pictures. One of our truck drivers was driving somewhere over here & Johnny happened to see our truck & stopped the driver. He asked our driver to give the pictures & message to me, and in the message asking me to send the pictures to your home, for he wouldn't have a chance to send them for a while. Let me know if you get the pictures.

Martha's brothers, George Boretsky (l.), 82nd Airborne Division, and John (r.),

2nd Armored Division, in Sicily, July 1943.

The fellow with the mustache in the picture is Augie's friend & was

with him when Augie visited me in Sicily. The pictures Johnny & I

took in Africa are ruined as Johnny told me in the message.

Johnny later found some undamaged negatives and photos and sent them home.

Here is a few different places I've seen while in Africa:

Oran is where I had the large photos taken of myself. [Below]

Algiers is where I had the smaller photos taken. [Below]

> *[And I] have seen Constantine, Bizerte and a lot of other little*
> *towns.*
>
> *I hated Africa because of the heat & will be glad to get a little*
> *cold weather in the States.*

As a New Englander accustomed to cooler weather, Borys found it exceedingly diffi-cult to become acclimated to the desert's oppressive summer heat. On the other hand, he felt the people in Africa were great, especially the French. He recalled the couple in Oran that offered him and his buddy the generosity of their home. He was able to shave with hot water, bathe, and eat indoors. Borys felt the French couple treated him like a son.

Borys also had a high regard for the British. From his battle experience with them, he believed they were terrific fighters and was glad the US and Great Britain were allies. Borys thought two words that aptly expressed his feelings towards the British were: "Rule Britannia."

> *Gee Martha Darling, I miss you ever so much. Just a matter of days*
> *& it'll be a year we've been apart Darling. I'll be a happy man to be*
> *with you again Darling, & won't even mind you bawling me out now*
> *and then. It can't be too long before we're together again Beloved,*
> *& I'm going to hang onto your apron strings just as our Patrica Ann*
> *will do.*
>
> *I can now say we've seen a bit of action while in Africa, nothing*
> *to be worried about. I hope your mail begins to catch up with me*
> *Darling, for I'm lonesome for you, & your mail while over here is*
> *all I look forward to let me know you're well, & at times I sit back to*

read it, imagining it's you Beloved talking to me. I've seen enough

of this side the world & I only look forward to being next to you

Darling.

All My Love, Loving You As Always,

Borys

In August, Borys received a few letters from Martha, including, to his amazement, her 1 August letter on 14 August—in only fourteen days! He replied to one of Martha's questions by saying, "No Darling, I didn't as yet get your letter you've sent for my birthday, expressing your Love for me. I guess a lot of your letters will never catch up with me." Additionally, Borys said, "I haven't received the letter of Mary telling me you were working in a bank as a clerk, and is the first I knew of your working. Am glad to hear your co-workers are very sociable, ... Also glad to hear you refused a job as a model." He told Martha he had written letters to her family, including Mary, Johnny, and Ann, who sent a small package containing ten packs of gum.

In his correspondence to Martha, Borys mentioned that when he receives mail from his family he gets, "... a kick from my brother Alek when he writes me. He describes his victory garden to me, & he gives me the sizes of different vegetables he grows in his victory garden. He's working helping some scrap iron dealer & says he makes around $15 a week."

The final bombing raid on the Palermo Harbor area occurred on 23 August. The air raid alert sounded at 0408 hours with an estimated twenty aircraft. German aircraft could see and sink two sub chasers and damage one coaster due to the lighting of the harbor with flares. Enemy losses attributed to the antiaircraft artillery fire were three planes—corrected from two on 30 September 1943 based on the interrogation of a prisoner of war (POW)—and one damaged due in part to illumination from searchlights of the Third Battalion. Allied night fighter planes were believed to have destroyed one aircraft, with one more probable.

On 31 August, an unusual order was received for the 62nd Coast Artillery Regiment to go on alert at a precise time. Men were forbidden within the revetment of any large gun or machine gun, so they could not engage any Axis plane in combat. To ensure this order was followed, an officer was stationed at each gun and would permit entrance by crewmembers only in case of aggressive action by the enemy.

An Italian plane landed at the Palermo airport, and peace negotiations took place. The discussions proved fruitful, as Italy capitulated three days later.

12

Sᴇᴘᴛᴇᴍʙᴇʀ 1943

Palermo, Sicily

The British Eighth Army invaded Italy on 3 September under cover of voluminous naval fire and Allied air support; the British and Canadians crossed the narrow Strait of Messina and hit the Italian province of Calabria. On that day, the Italian government signed a secret armistice that was to take effect on 8 September; the armistice was not announced until it took effect.

The American Fifth Army, under General Mark Clark, made its assault on 9 September at Salerno, which is south of Naples.

The retreating Germans took refuge behind a formidable barrier called the Gustav Line, stretching the width of the Italian peninsula. Due to the German strategic high-ground advantage, a stalemate resulted that lasted months.

As combat increased in Italy, enemy bombing missions stopped in Sicily. This enabled the Germans to concentrate their resources on the immediate threat that the Allies posed to their stranglehold on the Italian mainland. Therefore, the 62nd Coast Artillery Antiaircraft Regiment did not participate in defensive action in September 1943. Instead, they would go on the offensive against an aerial enemy that had plagued them since July—millions of flies.

Absent from the letters Borys wrote to Martha were the harsh conditions he was exposed to in Sicily, such as an overabundance of flies, the lack of any plumbing facilities and housing, and other unsanitary conditions. Flies got into the GIs food and mouths. These aggressive pests feasted on the soldiers when other food was not available.

Soldiers and civilians killed as a result of battle were buried as soon as possible, but animal carcasses such as horses and cows still littered the countryside. The US Army made repeated requests to Sicilian authorities to improve sanitary conditions and assisted in cleaning the dead animals in the occupied area; however, manure from livestock still provided breeding grounds for vermin. Instead of burying animal waste, the locals amassed it in large piles. Once again, the army solved the problem by bulldozing trenches to bury the dung. The citizens began to comply with sanitation requests, which reduced the fly population but did not eliminate it.

GIs also assisted with the removal of rubble from bombed-out buildings. Borys and his buddy, Bob Pollock, accumulated a stockpile of wood and put their construction skills to good use by building a hut for shelter instead of a pup tent. Providing more comfort than the tent, other soldiers built huts, and a small shanty town grew.

As mid-September approached, Borys wrote Martha:

My Dearly Beloved Martha,

> *... It's been a long while since I've got a letter from anyone, & I hope my mail going back is being received regularly. I haven't written to you for about a week Darling, this being my first letter. Tell my mom I'll write her a V letter shortly. It's past a year we've been apart*

Darling, & it's been an awful lonesome year being away from you Dearest. It's so slow that I lose track of time & days, but I do know that each day gone by is one day closer to going back to you, & is the only day I look forward to. We're kept pretty busy, but still time drags.

... How is Lizzie enjoying her vacation? Or I should have said how did she enjoy her vacation, before being now in School.

I hope you've received the pictures that John asked me to send, also the pictures I've sent of myself. The weather here is now getting somewhat cooler, & before long we'll be wearing overcoats....

I was wishing from the beginning of this year that I could be with you Dearest for Christmas, & I still haven't lost hope, for there's still a little over 3 months from now. Beloved this is the only present I could ever now enjoy is to be with you on Christmas Eve.

I took a hot shower today, the first since last June. I've taken a lot of baths between times but all cold water. It's a luxury to get hot water over here, so Darling, don't think me foolish if I spend an hour in a bath tub when we're married, & darling the bed will be pretty occupied on my time off....

If you could possibly send chocolates, I'd very much like to get them, & if I do get them remind me to kiss you for it some day, & if I can't get them I'll just kiss you anyway Dearest, for your sweet enough for me.

All My Undying Love, Loving You Forever,
Martha My Beloved, Only Yours,
Borys

At the end of September, an Italian bomber pilot of a Cant Z.1007 airplane, whose rank was first lieutenant, provided intelligence information to American officers upon questioning. He provided this account of the Axis raid on Palermo, Sicily, in August:

> *On August 4th they again bombed the port [Palermo] with 11 Cant Z 1007 and eighteen (18) Ju-88's bombers from Foggio Airdrome. They expected barrage firing and to their surprise it was radio [radar] controlled. The Italian formation did not get a chance to drop their loads on the port and jetted the bombs in the sea. They had to jettison their bombs because two of the aircraft were hit direct by flak, and exploded with full bomb load. Another aircraft crashed into a mountain near Bocca Di Falco and one aircraft crashed near the island of Vatica. Two aircraft were badly damaged and limped for Italy but crews had to bail out of both, and both aircraft crashed into the sea. One aircraft was shot down while going over the harbor and crashed about two (2) miles from Palermo.*
>
> *The Italian pilot stated that the German Air Force regarded the flak in the Palermo sector as the most accurate flak they have encountered in all their bombings over Palermo, Bizerte, Oran, and Sousse. He also remarked that the German Air Force is deadly afraid of Beaufighter aircraft.*

The defensive teamwork provided by the American antiaircraft artillerymen and British fighters during attacks provided proof that the Luftwaffe's (German air force) fears were valid.

September 1943 saw a resumption of German U-boat attacks. Their submarines took a beating during the second quarter of 1943, and there was a lull in U-boat activity that summer. However, a wolf pack of at least fifteen U-boats hit a westbound convoy on 19 September. This resulted in a running fight lasting four and a half days, whereby the US lost a small number of merchant ships and three escort vessels, and the Germans lost a larger number of subs. In actuality, according to the British, "Our estimate is that at least three U-Boats were sunk and six seriously damaged. Three escort vessels and six merchant vessels were sunk."

13

October 1943

Palermo, Sicily

My Dearest Martha,

Just a few lines letting you know I'm feeling fine. I miss you very much and am asking you not to worry about anything, please. I really couldn't say much when I left you excepting I loved you with all my heart and hope and will prove that love to you someday....

Tell Elizabeth I dreamt I found some dust in the parlor behind the radio and tell her not to take it to serious....

There isn't much I can think to write of right now, excepting to take care of yourself, and please don't go out by yourself nights (please) will you do that for me just as you promised me....

Tell Mickey I'm sorry I took a few good nights sleep from him by using his bed when I came to visit you.

Sleeping in the Boretsky home was a long-ago blessing compared to the hard, damp, and cold ground in Brooklyn, New York's Prospect Park, Africa, and now Sicily.

Earlier, Borys had written about difficulty in getting photos in Sicily and said of the ones he did obtain, "The pictures didn't come out to well, but anyway it resembles me."

Borys in 1943 Sicily.

Martha Darling, take a good look at the picture, for he's going to be your husband and he doesn't want to disappoint you.

Does he meet your approval Darling?

If he has any faults, I know you can correct them, for you're the only person he believes in and will listen to.

My mother writes that she may go to Brooklyn to visit my sister Sue for Christmas. I hope you can see her because you treated my mom swell the last time and she enjoyed her visit.

Until I hear from you I'll close with all my love, my sincerest love to you Martha Darling, and my best wishes for your health and happiness.

God bless your sweet heart.

Loving You As Ever,

Borys

October saw the World Series played with the American League's New York Yankees beating the National League's Saint Louis Cardinals four games to one, the exact reverse of the 1942 World Series. Martha's favorite team was victorious.

Martha and Borys bet their twenty-five kisses on the outcome of the Series itself, and not the Pennant, although neither would have objected if they had had to pay the other fifty kisses instead of twenty-five. As it was, Borys now owed Martha fifty kisses—twenty-five from 1942 and, of course, twenty-five from the 1943 World Series. Martha owed Borys twenty-five kisses for the birth of her nephew, John.

With thoughts of baseball on his mind, Borys finished writing his letter to Martha for the night, went outside the pup tent for fresh air, and headed over to the gun crew gathered about fifty feet away. He said to Robert Pollock, a Bostonian, "What do you think are the chances of the Sox winning the World Series next year?"

"Very good," he answered.

Overhearing the conversation, Lake said, "No way. The Dodgers will beat them in six games, if they're lucky enough to make it that far."

"I hope not," Borys said. "I want to collect twenty-five kisses from Martha."

Then Ira Goldman, another cannoneer and native of Bronx, New York, said, "Next year there'll be another Subway Series between the Yankees and Dodgers, just like 1941."

"No way," came a duet from Borys and Pollock.

"The Red Sox won the Series in 1918, when I was born, and they're overdue; 1944 will be a Sox victory year," Borys said.

"The Red Sox won't win another World Series this century," Lake said doubtfully.

The loss of baseball, football, and other sports enjoyed by Americans at home was a deprivation the servicemen had to suffer for the war's duration. Missed even more, of course, were their loved ones who worried about the servicemens' lives and safety.

Luck in the defense of the Palermo Harbor area continued in October 1943, since there were no air raids. But the cannoneers feared they would be drawn into battle from Sicily to the Italian mainland.

14

November 1943

Palermo, Sicily

In November 1943, training intensified to hone the regiment's expertise in weapon usage. Each battery had target practice for a period of ten days atop Monte Pellegrino, which included a plane towing a sleeve for the 40-mm, .50-caliber, and 90-mm guns.

One afternoon after training concluded, Pollock asked Borys about his experience in the prewar army since he was one of the few men in the regiment who had served then.

"I joined the army in mid-August 1938 and started training on the bigger guns: eight-, ten-, and twelve-inch guns. On Great Gull Island, there was even one sixteen-inch gun. About a month later, without warning, a violent hurricane hit Fishers Island in Long Island Sound, where Fort H. G. Wright is located. The gun crew was in the bunker as the wind howled at over a hundred miles per hour, torrential rains saturated everything in the open, and the ocean surged onto land. We could see more and more of the island becoming flooded, swallowed by the Atlantic, with trees washed away and any man-made structure reclaimed by the ocean. After several hours of pounding the vicinity of our position, the water came right up to the parapets, and things looked really bad. As the hurricane continued, we were fearful of the worst. Hours later, the winds waned and so did the flooding until the storm ended."

Not only did the 1938 Hurricane strike Long Island itself and the islands in the Sound, it also devastated coastal areas of surrounding states. For example, downtown Providence, Rhode Island, was flooded under several feet of ocean water; that storm killed hundreds of people in the northeast.

Borys came much closer to death on 16 February 1940. He had pain in his lower-right belly, fever, chills, and weakness. When he reported to the fort hospital, he had surgery for acute appendicitis. Borys was near death when the operation took place, since his appendix had burst and the poison had spread throughout his system. If it wasn't for the surgical skill of the colonel who completed the procedure, Borys would have died.

The extreme seriousness of his condition resulted in a ten-week recuperation period; that meant Borys had his three-year enlistment period extended by ten weeks to October 1941. Five months later, he met Martha.

The November 1943 Thanksgiving was the second one Borys had to endure without Martha. As consolation for his loneliness, Borys wrote Martha a poem:

> *My heart began to throb one day,*
> *Little did I know it was nature's way,*
> *To tell me I've found my love in life,*
> *And in that love a happiness and wife.*

> *As I gazed into her sparkling eyes,*

A light shone forth and I realized,

The sparkle in your eyes was like the stars above,

And in that sparkle I saw our love.

You looked at me in that sweet sort of way,

And in that look I could hear you say,

I too have found a love so true,

And my heart and life belong to you.

You have my heart and only you know,

That in my heart will always flow,

My undying love to only you,

Forever and ever I'll always be true.

You are so sweet and dear to me,

And I know forever you will always be,

The only girl I'll ever love,

Just as God watches from above.

The days go on and the time draws near,

Together we'll be once again my dear,

Together forever we'll never part,

Always forever you have my heart.

A November 1943 mail call brought Borys several letters from home. Borys received a letter from Martha stating that she had filled their US Treasury–approved stamp album with ten-cent savings stamps and had made war bond purchases with the stamps, other funds Borys had sent via his mother, and salary from her job.

Martha and Borys felt the savings bonds were a great investment, paying interest on the principal.

Now that she was eighteen, Martha would participate in the Sixth War Loan Drive in 1944 and receive a certificate from the US Treasury War Finance Committee, which commissioned her a second lieutenant in the Blue Star Brigade (civilians selling war bonds) "for outstanding patriotic endeavor and accomplishment in the sale of War Bonds." Martha also participated in the 1945 Seventh War Loan Drive, achieved a greater dollar-value sale of war bonds, and was commissioned a first lieutenant in the Blue Star Brigade.

Bond sales provided funds to finance the war effort. They also provided the purchaser with a savings incentive and, at the same time, reduced purchasing power to assist in keeping inflation under control. After the war, the redemption of bonds would stimulate consumer spending for an economy that had transitioned to peacetime pursuits. Issuing bonds in the bearer's name provided security if lost, stolen, or destroyed since bonds could be replaced. The sale of US war bonds from 1940 (when they were referred to as defense bonds) to 1946 resulted in the sale of roughly $185 billion to eighty-five million Americans.

Another letter, this one from his sister Sue in Brooklyn (as provided by Borys's niece, Anna), started a bit unusual but offered insight into the rationing situation stateside:

Dear Butch,

Shhhh!

I have a secret to tell you but you have to promise not to tell anyone else. Okay?

My daughter, Anna, was walking home from school with my neighbor Beth since it was her turn to pick up the children. As they passed the butcher shop, Tom, our butcher, called her into the store and whispered into her ear. Anna ran out of the store, across 4th Avenue, down Pacific Street, up the stairs of our house and into the kitchen with Beth and her daughter following.

She yelled, "Mommy, mommy."

Anna waved her hand above her head with a downward motion; I went to her, bent over and listened as she whispered, "Four pork chops," into my ear.

Knowing exactly what that meant, I took Anna by the hand and we ran back to the butcher shop to collect our four pork chops set-aside by Tom.

Sue's letter focused on meat rationing. Many other items were rationed during WWII, such as gasoline, coffee, and sugar. Rationing was a worldwide event and most nations enforced it to a greater degree than the US.

15

December 1943

Palermo, Sicily

There were no air raids or alerts in December. Because the 62nd AAA Regiment's mission remained the same, intensive target practice for the 40-mm, .50-caliber, and 90-mm guns continued throughout the month and included the use of radar control for the big guns. Overall, the regiment saw significant improvements in all aspects of gun and fire-control usage.

December's days grew shorter and its nights expanded—indications of a waning year and the approaching holidays. Borys dreamt of his love, Martha, who was constantly in his thoughts:

My Dearest Darling Martha,

Well here it is with only 3 more shopping days to Christmas, and I've nothing to shop for here...

Martha Darling, I pray we will be together next Christmas with you as my wife.

I've written a letter to my sister and asked her to tell you to send me if you possibly could some candy, gum and some toilet articles, especially a few tooth brushes & tooth paste because I've just about run out of everything and it's almost impossible to get them things here, so I'll leave everything up to you Darling, because you could always figure out what I needed most, (including you).

I'm well and still healthy, and about the only thing I constantly think of is you, Martha Darling. Are you well & happy? Please let me know Darling.

Gee Darling for the first time in my life I've found true love & happiness with you, and I've got to give you that happiness in return. I thank God for giving your love & for making me want to live to return that love (my love) & happiness to you....

I guess you know me pretty darn well by now Darling, but I just can't help but loving you. Every time you look at me with that twinkle in your eye-Oh well any way, Patrica will be the result, (Our Patrica) when I see you again, and you get that twinkle in your eye. I can only look forward to have you as my wife and I can only say I'm the luckiest guy in the world to have a girl like you. I wish right now I could hold you in my arms and whisper my love for you in your ear.

How is your Mom & Pop, give them both my love & also give my love to their Daughter Martha. Has my mom visited you? Tell them again I'm well and have written 3 letters to them... Do you go to show much? I'll bet you sit more comfortably in show now, without me falling asleep on your shoulder. I'm now closing praying this letter reaches you and finds you well & happy, With all my love to you Martha Sweetheart Darling.

God Bless you all.

I'm wishing you a very Merry Christmas and a Happy New Year.

Loving You Always Forever Yours, Love Again,

Borys

'Twas Christmas Eve within a large wall tent where the soldiers had gathered in celebration with an abundance of liquor, or "good Christmas spirits," as the GIs put it. It was a much-appreciated occasion for sharing personal reminiscences. The artillerymen talked about the time they were bivouacked in Brooklyn, New York's Prospect Park. Borys spoke:

"Hey Lake, did I ever tell you about the time Martha got challenged in Prospect Park by a sentry of ours?" Borys asked.

"No, what happened?"

"It was about a month after we met, and at the end of April 1942, I informed Martha I'd be on duty at the top of Prospect Park's Lookout Hill that night. Martha thought she'd surprise me and left her home just after sunset. She'd been to the top of Lookout Hill many times. She entered the park through the Sixteenth Street entrance.

"Although it was dark, she found her way to the hill's staircase by the approach to Center Drive. As she climbed the steps leading to the gun position, she heard the sound of her leather soles scuffing against the slate steps; all else was quiet. About halfway to the top of the hill, someone challenged her with 'Halt! Who goes there? Friend or foe?' Startled, she said, 'Friend.' Someone shined a flashlight in her face, causing her to squint.

"Martha heard the sound of the hill's soil crunching beneath army boots as a soldier approached her. He asked Martha, still shining the light in her face, 'Ma'am, what are you doing here?' She said, 'I came to see my boyfriend, who's stationed on an ack-ack gun at the top of the hill.' He said, 'I'm sorry, ma'am, but no civilians are allowed on the hill. I can give him a message later if you like.' She said, 'No, thank you. I'll see him tomorrow.' Then she turned and went home. The next day when Martha saw me, she told me the story and added that she hadn't left a message because she would've given my name, and she didn't want to get me in trouble."

Martha told of an incident just before Borys shipped overseas, in August 1942, going to Farrell's Bar in Brooklyn with part of Martha's family—Johnny, George, and Jimmy. They went there after sunset, about 9:00 p.m., and stayed late. The guys were buying drinks, since Borys was the first to go overseas. A couple of hours later, Johnny ordered a round and gulped a mug of beer when—pow!—he took a shot to the back of the head.

Johnny turned to see who hit him and was dragged, by his left ear, off the barstool by his mother. She then slapped George in the back of the head with her left hand and dragged him, by his right ear, off his barstool.

As she hauled them out the ladies' entrance on Sixteenth Street, she said, "Get home!" Then Jimmy got another round for himself and Borys. The bartender asked him to settle the bill, which Jimmy did, but he told the bartender not to worry because those were her sons and the two of them were going to stay even though it was near midnight. The bartender said, "I don't think so." Borys looked in the mirror over the bartender's shoulder just as Mom planted her left hand across her son-in-law's skull and her right hand on Borys. Mom yanked them off their barstools and, with a heave-ho, pulled them out of the bar by their ears. Once they were out on Sixteenth Street, they got the same stern lecture—"Get home!"—which they obliged.

Borys said of the incident, "Boy, us he-men certainly moved out of that bar fast when Mom strong-armed us."

As 1943 drew toward its close, Borys joined the rest of the world in praying for peace.

16

Januar 1944

Palermo, Sicily

From the third through the sixth of January, the 62nd Coast Artillery Regiment (Antiaircraft) 90-mm guns began field artillery target practice. Both the First and Second Battalions began antimechanized firing practice on 10 January and continued to 14 January.

It seemed to Borys and other cannoneers that the nature of their mission might change. This was the consequence of the destruction of a large segment of enemy aircraft by antiaircraft fire and fighter interception. AAA outfits would have their secondary role come to the forefront—that of field artillery. The belief that the antiaircraft artillerymen now had was that they were to join battle on the Italian mainland, especially since this was another month in which no air raids occurred.

With love in his heart and Martha on his mind, Borys wrote:

My Dearly Beloved Martha,

It's Sunday evening and a swell sun is beginning to set in the western sky. I was just thinking Martha Darling, west is the direction I'll be traveling some day to get back to you. When that time for the voyage back comes I'll be a happy man knowing I have you Darling to go back to, and marry, and live the happiness with you over again, just as we've lived it before we parted.

Gee Martha Darling, it's all I look forward to, is to be in your arms again, and love you and kiss your sweet tender lips. I could just hug you and will as soon as I get you back in my arms. You just wait and see Martha Darling, for telling me you love me, I'm going to kiss you until your lips are burning from me pressing mine against them ever so tight. You see Martha Darling, you'll just have to forgive me when you're in my arms again, and with the both of us loving each other the way we do, well Darling I'll put it this way, our marriage will tell the story. I'll bet our Patrica Ann won't be as pretty as her pretty mommy Martha....

I wrote Mary a few days ago and have written Johnny yesterday.

Believe it or not Darling, Johnny and I turned out to be the best of friends.

When Johnny and I first met, in a way I now realize, I couldn't blame him for being a little wary of me. You are his sister and as I've once told you Darling, and as Johnny perhaps had in his mind, that service men and even the majority of civilian males will go with any girl, not for love, but what they can get out of a girl and then leave them for some other girl.

So you see Beloved, I can't blame Johnny at the time for being a little wary towards me, because he didn't seem to understand I loved you when we were first going together.

The first time I knew I was in love with you was when we met at the dance and we went out on the park bench and I was hoping for

a kiss... you were afraid Johnny would see. I knew I'd have to work

hard to win your love...

Borys met Martha 25 March 1942 while stationed with the 62nd AAA in Prospect Park, Brooklyn, New York. He believed she was on her way to work that morning and he asked Martha to a dance the army was sponsoring that evening. When Martha asked her parents for permission to date Borys, her mother was agreeable. What made the Boretsky men extremely guarded about this date was that Borys was a soldier—a *soldier*! Johnny, also a soldier but in the Second Armored Division, had heard some wild stories of soldiers dating. Martha could only meet Borys at the dance in the Prospect Park Picnic House if Johnny was her chaperone. With Martha's agreement, the date was on and the "wary" Johnny also met Borys that evening.

I am also lonesome without you. I pray that God Almighty protect

and keep you happy until I come back to you so I can take that lone-

someness and replace it with my love and happiness.

With All My Undying Love To You Martha Dearest Darling,

Loving You Forever,

Borys

On 22 January 1944, the Fifth Army circumvented the Gustav Line by landing and establishing a beachhead north of the Gustav Line and south of Rome in the Anzio sector; they caught the Germans off guard. While the invasion troops hesitated for several days, German divisions commenced a counteroffensive. The delay resulted in the rescue group getting butchered on the beaches of Anzio; they failed to seize the high ground before the Germans poured in reinforcements.

The Alban Hills are only five to ten miles from the beaches and it was very likely that US troops could have been in Rome within weeks since it was only thirty or forty miles north of Anzio.

17

Fᴇʙʀᴜᴀʀʏ 1944

Palermo, Sicily

From 10–18 February, field artillery firing practice continued, with the Long Toms improving their hit ratio.

Borys's letters to Martha included such sentences as "I was reminiscing about our dating in the summer of 1942. Just then, we assembled for mail call. I nervously held my breath in anticipation of a letter from you. My name was called and, thankfully, one of the letters I received was yours."

My Own Dearest Beloved Martha,

Martha Darling, I've met you at a time when I never had anything, because I couldn't help it being in the army, I could never offer you much at the time. You stood by me knowing I was broke and my folks aren't wealthy and you still loved me and stood by me. I had nothing to offer you Martha my Darling, but my love. The day we're together again Darling, I'm going to do my best to give you things you really deserve Darling, as soon as my army discharge is given to me and we get married. Even on our engagement I had nothing to give you but my love. [Borys had to borrow the money to purchase Martha's engagement ring.] Believe me Martha Darling, it hurt me knowing I was broke and everyone else knew it. I felt bad but it didn't discourage me, because I loved you and knew you loved me and realized I had to work hard to give you everything to make you happy as my wife.

Yes Martha Darling, you love me and stood by me, regardless of what anyone thought. You're so sweet and Dear to me, Dearest Beloved Martha that I wouldn't or don't care for anyone, because I have your love & you have all my undying Love and our happiness. No one or anything will ever come between us and our love Martha Darling. The day will come Darling and we'll be together again, but this time we'll be together as man and wife with our little home, our love and our happiness and our family, & our Patrica Ann to be forever happy....

I remember one of the first times we met when we made a date and I waited on 9th Avenue and 15th Street. You were late and I waited in the snow and rain looking for you, Martha my Darling. After a while, you came out of the subway with Lizzie as I was standing across the street on the corner by the drug store.

I was mad while waiting but forgot all about it when you came out of the subway. It was a good thing too since that was the first time you brought me home to meet your family. It was also the first time I talked with your mom over a cup of coffee. I sure do miss her and our conversations.

I wish I could send my ration of coffee to your mom.

Tell your mom I just made a cup of coffee on a small kerosene stove I bought in Africa. I used to buy eggs from Arab farmers and fry them on the stove....

Your mom made sure I was never hungry – she made sure her beautiful daughter did not get a starved husband.

Thank your mom and pop for bringing a girl as sweet and beautiful into this world as you Martha.

As long as I have you Martha Darling, your love, our home and Patrica Ann with perhaps one or 2 more additions to our family, is all I want in this life. For with all of that I'll always be happy & contented.

I wished I were with you Darling and the war were over now, I could be working and we could be setting our wedding day. It won't be to long Martha Darling, so please don't worry....

Loving You Forever,

All My Undying Love, Only Yours,
Borys

The USAAF's (United States Army Air Force) priority became the total destruction of the German Luftwaffe before the invasion of France and the opening of the second front. Therefore, in early 1944, the bombers, with long-range fighter escorts, concentrated their attacks on airfields, aircraft-manufacturing facilities, and oil refineries to force the Luftwaffe to defend them. These raids were suspended during the last quarter of 1943 due to sizeable bomber losses. The new and superior US P-51 Mustang fighter devastated the Luftwaffe, with more than 450 German planes shot down during the week of 20–26 February 1944 alone. This week, which became known as Big Week, was an all-out effort on the part of the Allies to destroy Germany's aircraft and industry. The Allies now controlled the skies over Europe.

18

In 1943, the army began to reorganize coast artillery antiaircraft regiments into group headquarters and separate battalions for the guns (90-mm), automatic weapons, and searchlight battalions to improve efficiency. The group, replacing the regiment, was already in use in tank formations. In March 1944, the 62nd Coast Artillery Regiment reorganized as follows:

- The 62nd regimental headquarters became the 80th AAA group headquarters
- The 62nd First Battalion became the 62nd AAA Gun Battalion
- The 62nd Second Battalion became the 893rd AAA Automatic Weapons Gun Battalion
- The 62nd Third Battalion became the 331st AAA Searchlight Battalion

Later in the war, while in France and Germany, the AAA Gun Battalion would see attachment (temporary assignment) to different groups/organizations as circumstances dictated. Because Borys was an artilleryman on a Battery C gun, part of the First Battalion, he remained with the 62nd AAA Gun Battalion. With the reorganization of their outfit, the antiaircraft artillerymen were now certain they would be sent to the Italian mainland to join battle there.

Borys continued to woo Martha with sentimental letters:

My Own Dearest Darling Martha,

I dreamt about you again Martha Darling and not being next to you hurts.

Martha Darling, as soon as I'm back, we'll get your wedding ring – one to sort of match your engagement ring.

I wrote you the beginning of this month asking if you remembered last year, our first anniversary, when I asked you to play the Blue Danube on your sister's recorder?

I said we should do the same for our second anniversary. We can re-live the moment of our first dance to the Blue Danube Waltz. I believe it would be swell for both of us if you play it on March 25th, at 6:00 PM, New York time.

At that time, I will hum the Blue Danube wherever I am and imagine I'm dancing with you as you listen to it and imagine you are dancing with me.

What a wolf I turned out to be with you, but believe me Martha Darling, I just can't help it for I love you so much, and as you know you just made me want to hold you and love you.

You see Darling it's this way with me, I couldn't have more happiness no matter what I had in this world, just you and your Love is all I want and that's happiness for me.

I Love You Darling and only until the Day that I can have you in my arms as my wife to love, will I be happy.

…sent Mary a V letter letting her know I got the package with the gum and candies and also got your letter…

I'm now kissing your kisses of lipstick on the letter Darling. I'm going to get the real kisses from you Martha Darling very soon, your kisses that burn with love & makes me never want to let you go... Your kisses of lipstick on each letter are sweet Darling, and it makes me feel good to know even though just a print of your lips, it was put on by a feeling of your love for me through your heart. I kiss each kiss over and over just as if it were you there Martha Darling....

Martha Darling, I don't care who knows or reads this letter, because I Love you Dearly and Love you above anything on this earth. My heart bleeds its love for you Martha Darling, and I yearn and pray constantly that your well and I can be back to you as soon as possibly, to marry you Darling and do my best to give you happiness.

You're beautiful Martha Darling and I noticed you still have your natural hair style, just as the night I parted from you, and just as I have my natural wave, or at least you my Darling say it's a natural wave.

I'm not worried as I know you are waiting and we'll make up for the time apart.

After we're married and you see that twinkle in my eyes – you better hide because – well anyway... Mm Mm.

Martha Dearest, you can't keep me up late because I have to put in a hard days work. I'm kidding Martha as we had swell times coming home early in the morning.

I go on sentry duty in another half hour. The stars are out and I'll be thinking of you during my tour of guard.

Loving You As Ever,

My Everlasting Love to You,

Borys

19

Aᴘʀɪʟ 1944

Palermo, Sicily

As April progressed, the cannoneers continued field artillery firing practice, which included the performance of maintenance on the Long Tom. With the preparation for the invasion of a yet-unknown area of Europe, they took time to clean and paint their M1A1 90-mm gun. It was of the greatest importance to the gun crew that their cannon function properly.

Borys reminisced about asking Martha's parents for their approval to marry her:

April 1ˢᵗ 1944—7:00 P.M.

My Own Dearly Beloved Martha,

Here it is the ending of another day & the beginning of a new month...

Martha Darling you make me ever and ever so happy just saying you love me.

I received Easter cards from you, your folks, and my family. It sure was swell getting all them cards. Thank you Darling and thank your family.

Just got your package Darling, containing the candy…

I remember when I asked your mother first about marriage since I knew she was aware we loved each other. I figured mom would just explain to your pop and everything would be okay. Yep, I really thought I would get away with asking your father for your hand in marriage easy.

Instead, mom said I should tell him personally, boy did I get shaky.

I thought pop would hit me with the table but I just got a little lecture and then got his consent. With that, we could plan for our future and marriage….

Gee Darling, I'm going to work hard and love it, to come home every night from work and have you and Patrica waiting with supper and to have you two to work for, to love, and to enjoy living for. Martha Darling, I've always dreamed & thought of having this, and throughout my life I had that empty feeling, trying to reach for that something I could never seem to find to fill in that empty feeling. Then I met you Martha Darling, as if fate put it that way and got a strange feeling. And a few days later I realized my dream had become a reality. I had found that something I've always lacked and wanted, and then realized I had fallen in love & it could only be you that could fulfill my dreams….

About the only thinking I do here is of you Martha Darling, and picture you making my breakfast and supper, going to work and coming from work, and nights being next to you listening to the radio and occasionally or I should say very occasionally trying to steal a kiss from you. Some nights taking in a movie or visiting dif-

ferent people together. But as soon as we have our Patrica Ann we'll always be home nights, changing diapers.

So your pop painted the kitchen and put a new linoleum on the floor. I'll buy pop a drink or since he did such a good job, I'll buy him a quart providing he can sneak me a few drinks on the quiet without you knowing. I have another plan to sneak a few drinks without you or your mom knowing it, but I won't let you know because you'll be wise to me.

Ever lasting love,

Loving You Forever Only You,
Borys

An April mail call brought Borys a letter from home dated the beginning of March. His brother Alex had written that he would plant his victory garden with tomatoes that would grow as large as pumpkins and as red as fire engines. Borys wrote back to his parents that he always got a kick out of Alex's writing.

April 1944 saw the start of another baseball season and the renewed rivalry between the Yankees and Red Sox. Of course, that meant the accompanying rivalry between Martha and Borys with each rooting for their favorite team. In truth, it didn't really matter which team won because Martha and Boys were both winners in love.

It appeared that the Allies would be winners too, but the war still had a long way to go.

The bomber campaign against the Nazi oil infrastructure commenced. The US Eighth Air Force from British bases concentrated on the synthetic oil plants north of Munich. The US Fifteenth Air Force from Foggia, Italy, targeted synthetic oil facilities in Prussia and Nazi-occupied countries, including Rumania.

20

May 1944

Palermo, Sicily

By May 1944, the antiaircraft artillerymen's field artillery firing practice approached perfection. The German Wehrmacht (armed forces) would suffer devastating results in France, most notably the Colmar Pocket, and the German homeland.

In anticipation of her birthday the following month, Borys wrote a poem to Martha:

We walk together in Life's sweet Path

Never to fear Human Wrath

We walk as one in Human Life

And never fear, this Human strife

Our Love grows stronger as time goes by

Our Love United will never Die

We walk as one, as our Dear Lord Hath said

Life's short path is our bed

I can not say how strong my Love

Willst ever be, as our Lord's white Dove

My Heart is but a memory

Forever my love will always be

And in our Hearts we beat as one

And Shine Forever as God's radiant Sun

...Gee Darling, I wished I could be with you tonight to tell you I Love You. Please do your best Martha Darling & plan for our home and marriage, for when I get back to you Darling, my heart just can't wait to be your husband....In my moms letter to me, she says you're pretty & she'll be happy to have you as her daughter in law. Love to your mom, from her future son in law, on this past Mother's Day....

I'm lonesome Martha Darling, lonesome for you & your love. I'm just thinking Martha my Darling, I'm going to give you a gift after we're married & you're going to give me a gift. Guess what? I may as well tell you Darling for you'd be wondering. Here it is Darling, Patrica Ann. It'll be a cute little bundle to present me with Darling. Gee Martha Darling, that's all I ask and want out of this life is you Darling, our own little family and home.

All My Undying Love, Martha My Beloved,

All My Love, Loving You As Always,

Borys

On 9 May 1944, Allied forces used fourteen divisions to attack the Gustav Line's west coast from the Tyrrhenian Sea to Cassino, Italy. It was their fourth attempt to break through these tough German defenses. US and British forces struck at Monte Cassino on 12 May 1944, aided by air power, and within a week, had taken it and several other towns. On 18 May, Polish troops took Monastery Hill at Cassino, in the Gustav Line's center.

On 23 May, the push out of the Anzio beachhead pocket began to benefit from total air dominance, which assisted in the breakout by 25 May. On that day, the main Allied force from the Gustav Line linked with the Anzio forces. The Fifth Army battled the Germans in the Alban Hills and took Mount Peschio on 1 June, followed by Rome on 4 June.

The skies over Palermo continued to remain free of hostile aircraft. Soon, however, the antiaircraft artillerymen would enter harm's way.

21

JUNE 1944

Palermo, Sicily

Operation Overlord, the invasion of the beaches at Normandy, France, launched on 6 June. The second front in Europe opened, much to the Russians' relief and the Germans' grief.

American Airborne Divisions parachuted into France at 0130 hours, several hours ahead of landings from the six-thousand-ship invasion fleet. The British and Canadians landed near Caen while the Americans came ashore farther west and on the Cotentin Peninsula, closer to the deep-water port of Cherbourg.

Two days later, the beachheads were secure, and Allied troops pushed north to the strategic port of Cherbourg and captured its port on 27 June. The Nazis destroyed much of the harbor before surrendering to the Allies. The Allies had thousands of ships and hundreds of thousands of men, overwhelming the enemy forces on the beaches. In the first twenty-four hours, sixty-six thousand GIs landed; within a week, nearly 250,000 GIs were in France.

Air superiority was key; over ten thousand Allied bomber and fighter aircraft attacked Nazi troop concentrations and motor convoys. Other aircraft, such as glider and transport planes, supplemented the American and British combat air fleet. The combined air, naval, and ground forces enabled the Allies to secure beachheads within days of the commencement of operations against the supposedly impregnable Nazi Atlantic wall in France.

To develop an enormous air armada, American aircraft plants in such cities as San Diego, Seattle, Wichita, and Willow Run, Michigan, produced almost three hundred thousand aircraft by the war's end at a cost to taxpayers of $45 billion, or roughly 25 percent of America's $183 billion munitions bill. In terms of 2024 dollars, this would be about $781 billion and roughly $3.176 trillion, respectively. The aircraft industry employed more than two million workers, of whom nearly half a million women worked in aircraft manufacturing.

Borys reminisced about one of his dates with Martha:

My Dearly Beloved Martha, My Love, My Darling Love,

Martha Darling, it's 10:00 in the morning and you must still be sleeping and I can picture your pretty head sunk in a feathered pillow. I would give anything to be next to you. I don't think it will be much longer when I'll be whispering my love for you in your ear instead of writing it.

...Got Mary's May 12th V letter & have sent her one a few days ago.... Martha Dearest Darling as soon as I get back to you I'll have to marry you as soon as possible, for I've got to have you, I've just got to have you Dearest for I can't live without you. I Love You Martha Darling & even though we're far apart your love for me & your kisses burn deep with my love for you in my heart.... Your

sweet Martha Darling and I Love You. I never lived until I met you Darling & I'll never live until the day I can be with you Martha Darling again.

Martha Darling, your letter was swell where you talk about our early dating.

We would sit on a park bench together at night to hold and kiss. I never wanted to stop kissing you or take you home since we were in our own little world.

The next night your mother would say, "Don't forget to be home early," and I would reply, "Yes, mom, early in the morning." Your mother took that lightly because she knew we were across the street on the park-side bench.

I was such an awful walk—I wanted to kiss and embrace you every time we were close.

The first night we are together again, I will hold you all night long. We'll have good times and live in that beautiful world of our own but this time as man and wife.

Martha Darling, I woke Bob last night in our pup tent and told him I dreamt we married.

He congratulated me, said to kiss the bride, rolled over and went back to sleep....

Got a letter yesterday from my mom... she will most likely visit Sue this summer, so please take her to anywhere she cares to go.... She says she will take some pictures with you. Please send a couple when they're developed, okay Darling.

I Love you Martha Darling and even though we're far apart, your love for me and your kisses burn deep with my love for you in my heart.

June 24th will be your birthday and about the only thing I can send you is my love, Martha Darling.

Have a very Happy, Healthy and Wonderful Birthday. I expect to give my personal birthday wishes along with dozens of kisses to you on your next birthday.

Loving You Forever Martha, Only Yours,

Loving You Always Forever Yours, Love Again,

Borys

Martha wrote on 16 June 1944, that her brother, Johnny, was mentioned on radio station WEAF. The news reported that in fighting around Carentan, France:

"The roads are littered with German dead, mowed down by the withering fire from our tanks. At least 500 dead Germans are piled up in the ditches and hedgerows. 'We gave 'em the garden hose', says Private Boretsky, referring to sixty thousand rounds of .30-caliber tank bullets. 'The yanks were hard-pressed there, and when the tanks rolled up to take on the krauts, they stood up and cheered—you'd have thought you were at a Giants-Dodgers game,' said Private Boretsky of Brooklyn."

22

JULY 1944

Palermo, Sicily, and Taranto, Mainland Italy

On 6 July 1944, the 62nd AAA Battalion departed Palermo for Taranto, the staging area, in preparation for the invasion of southern France. The GIs, however, were unaware of Operation Anvil (also known as Operation Dragoon), which would bring them to Marseilles, France, in August.

During the remainder of July 1944, the antiaircraft artillerymen prepared for the next invasion, which was still unknown to them. Until early June, they had strongly suspected they were destined for the Italian mainland, but the Normandy invasion cast doubt. Wherever the army sent them, they wanted to be prepared. The troops waterproofed guns, other matériel, and motor transport and prepared to load their equipment onto transports.

As July was ending, Borys's twenty-sixth birthday, 30 July, neared, and he wrote Martha once again expressing his deep love.

Borys indicated that the pen Martha had given him was "in bad shape and scratches awful." With the 62nd AAA Battalion's Sicilian position remaining static since the previous Christmas, the pen had seen a great deal of "action." Borys thanked Martha again for the practical gift and said, "Well Darling, it's not surprising with all the letters, V-mails and postcards I've sent that I would wear out a couple of pens."

Borys informed Martha that he had not heard from her or from home in a few weeks due to his move from Sicily to mainland Italy. He could not specify where in Italy because of censorship regulations and security. Borys expected it would be several weeks before the mail would catch up to him and reminded Martha, "If you don't get mail from me for a long time, please don't worry for any chance I have I'll always write you Darling." Borys asked her not to worry because "the war will be over some day Darling and I'll be back to you."

My Own Dearest Darling Martha,

As you once said you are branded in my life. We're both branded together as one, and nothing can ever come between us, because our love for each other will never die....

Night and day you are in my mind. About the only thing or enjoyment I have over here is thinking of you and the times we've been together and I constantly keep thinking of the times you and I will have once again when I can hold you in my arms and know I'm not dreaming, but only the next time we're together it will be as man and wife.

I can only say one thing Martha Darling, they can't have my life over here, because you'll bawl me out, so I'll have to give it to you, and nobody else but you!

After we are together, we'll plan our marriage because I have to marry you as soon as possible.

I have to have you Martha Darling, as my wife so I can work hard, love you, and live for the day we have planned. That day to share our love and happiness as one, Mrs. & Mr. Borys Bohun.

While I'm working and you shopping with perhaps your sister,

you will say what the heck can I get for supper for that hungry hus-
band of mine....

The pictures we took in Coney Island are fading from the rain
and weather.

Martha Dearest, I admire the ruby ring you gave me for my
birthday two years ago....

I love you ever and ever so much and want you to take pity on me
and send me an extra kiss.

Martha Darling, you have my heart so please take care of it.
Loyally and Faithfully Only Yours,

Loving You Always Forever,
Borys

There was little progress in Normandy during the first half of July, except for the Allied capture of Caen on 9 July and Saint-Lô on 19 July. To break out of the Normandy
area with its formidable defensive hedgerows (tree-covered dirt mounds), on 25 July,
the Allies committed eighteen hundred aircraft—fighters, dive-bombers, and medi-
um and heavy bombers—to bomb a five-by-one-mile-wide section west of Saint-Lô.
Four infantry divisions and two armored divisions smashed through the bombed area,
breaking the Nazi containment in Normandy on 26 July, and entered Brittany.

The tremendous industrial capability of the United States would result in the construction of almost three hundred thousand aircraft during World War II. American air
strength peaked in July 1944 with nearly eighty thousand planes in service, comprising

sixteen air forces within the USAAF. No Axis power could come close to reproducing the rate at which the US could replace damaged or destroyed aircraft, resulting in the dwindling air strength of its enemies. Hence, Allied air superiority played a vital role in destroying Axis industrial complexes and fuel supplies, which resulted in fuel consumption exceeding production.

During June and July in Italy, German forces withdrew northward to a point about one hundred miles north of Rome and stood fast at the nearly impregnable Gothic Line.

23

August 1944

Taranto, Naples, and Rome, Italy

Batteries C and D proceeded to the staging area at Naples, Italy, on 4 August. That same day, Headquarters Battery and Batteries A and B embarked at Brindisi, Italy, for Saint Tropez, France. They provided antiaircraft protection for the landing beaches beginning on 16 August.

On 20 August, Batteries A and B moved to La Londe-les-Maures, France. Field artillery missions destroyed two German observation posts. On 23 August, a concentrated cannonade at Fort Malque and the port area in Toulon knocked out Nazi observation towers and gun pits.

In the intervening time, the antiaircraft artillerymen of Battery C received leave to go to Rome the following day. Goldman, on sentry duty, got soaking wet during a sudden downpour. Ordinarily, the weather in this area is calm during summer, but, unfortunately for Goldman, conditions deteriorated badly during the night. He got Borys to relieve him while he quickly changed from his wet standard dress coveralls to his dry wool duty uniform and boots. After several moments, Goldman resumed duty, with no one else knowing of the substitution.

Before finishing his patrol, the rain started again and drenched Goldman from helmet to toe. Finally, after sunrise, he was relieved from duty and joined his team as the men were preparing for a short leave to Rome, Italy, just before their departure to France.

"I decided not to go," Goldman said.

"Why?" Lake asked.

"Because my uniforms and boots are all wet. The aerologist didn't predict any rain for last night, but it rained twice."

"Hey, wait a minute," Lake said. "You and Zarr are the only two in the squad the same size, and you had plans to go together. Zarr, why don't you lend Goldman your extra uniform and boots?"

Zarr hesitated a moment but agreed when Goldman said, "I'll buy drinks."

With the deal done and clothes and boots changed, the GIs began the trek for their Roman holiday.

Upon arrival in Rome, Borys and Pollock decided to go their separate ways in the morning and get together at noon in a prearranged spot. A few minutes early, Borys bought some postcards and then met Pollock. The men from Massachusetts spent the rest of the day touring Rome before returning to the truck and their battery.

Borys also used some of his leave time to write postcards on August 21, 1944, from Rome to family in the US.

Dearest Mother,

Here is a picture in Rome. Got a lot of cards so am sending them to everyone. Will write soon.

Love to All.

Borys

Borys wrote of the night he left Martha two years prior:

Dearest Beloved Martha,

I'm going to do my best to make you happy Martha Darling and will give you my sincerest love and try to make myself worthy of your beautiful love as my wife....

I'm now experiencing the bitterest moments of my life, being away from you Darling. They could give me the whole part of this world and I'd never be happy unless I had your love & you Martha Darling next to me.

You've only given me happiness Darling, and even as the night I left you at the subway, you're next to me, and will always be until the day I return to you to feel your kisses burn deep with love into me. The night we parted in the subway was hard for me to leave you and was the most bitterest moment in my life... As the train left everything kept revolving in my mind and could only see you in my mind. At all times I only think of you Darling & visualize our marriage & home & our Patrica Ann... It has been 2 years since that bitter time.

As the days go by, it is closer to our marriage. Gee Martha Darling, I miss you and your love and everything you did that made me happy, and the time is coming nearer when we'll both be together to always enjoy our love & happiness....

Why Martha Darling, I never knew I snored in the theatre when I used to fall asleep on your shoulder, at least I never heard myself snore. Darling the people certainly got their moneys worth to hear my musical snore. Darling when we go to the theatre again, I prom-

ise you I won't fall asleep. It'll be your turn to fall asleep on my shoulder, okay Darling....

I dreamt of kissing you last night and I'm on the level-it seemed real.

I know it's hard for you living in hopes and staking your whole future on me and I can't disappoint you Darling, for my only intention is to return to you to give and receive your love and try to give you the happiness you've given to me.

God Bless Your Sweet Little Heart Beloved, The Heart I Love and Forever will Love. Our Hearts will be one through our children, Martha My Beloved.

Loving You Always Martha Darling with All My Heart,
Borys

During late August, Batteries C and D made final preparations in waterproofing guns, motor transport, and other matériel as well as loading equipment onto transports; they joined their sister batteries in Marseilles, France, on 31 August.

The US Seventh Army successfully invaded southern France on 15 August and swept rapidly north through the Rhone Valley. The offensive was known as Operation Anvil.

Applying the same tactics they had used weeks before the Normandy invasion, the Allies bombed the designated landing area in southern France and several others to confuse the enemy of the true invasion site. Bridges, road junctions, and railways were bombed, which, in effect, isolated the region.

Before the landings, the Allied naval force had shelled enemy defenses along coastal landing areas as parachute troops dropped behind enemy lines and captured vital positions, just as commandos did in the predawn darkness. This assured a reduction in enemy opposition for the men in the landing operation.

After the landings, loyal Frenchmen in the French Forces of the Interior (FFI), underground groups known as the Marquis and the Franc-Tireurs, aided the Allies. The world witnessed the proud spirit of French citizens, with their love of liberty, methodically destroy the Nazi occupation forces, which gradually led to the victory France demanded. Even with all the support they received, the Seventh Army met Nazi resistance in Marseilles, especially in the French naval port of Toulon.

Mid-August also saw an Allied victory in northern France. An area near the town of Falaise became known as the Falaise Pocket. US troops moved on the Falaise area and encircled the Germans, who partially broke out during the third week of August in the region between Argentan and Falaise. A force of over one hundred thousand Germans retreating from the northern French coast was almost trapped between American, British, and Canadian troops. American artillery killed ten thousand enemy soldiers. The Allies took roughly fifty thousand prisoners, with about fifty thousand Germans escaping the Falaise Pocket and retreating behind the Seine River, thus ending the Battle for Normandy.

PART THREE:

SOUTHERN FRANCE

24

Sᴇᴘᴛᴇᴍʙᴇʀ 1944

Marseilles, France

The 62nd AAA Gun Battalion received M-4 tractors in September to replace the Prime Mover for their M1A1 90-mm guns. The M-4 tractors were better equipped to navigate muddy roads and winter's snow and ice.

Sergeant Peter Kaminski was the gun commander and firmly believed in working as a team; he instilled this concept into his soldiers. Kaminski assembled the gun crew on a drizzling September day.

"The battalion will receive M-4 tractors to replace the Prime Mover for our M1A1 90-mm guns," Kaminski said. He asked Zarr, "Can you drive a tractor?"

"I can drive anything with wheels, Sergeant Kaminski."

"Tractors have tracks like tanks, Zarr," Kaminski said. "If you can't drive one, I'll get someone else to drive."

Lake stepped forward and said, "I'll drive the tractor if he can't."

Pollock added, "I drove a tractor on my grandfather's farm."

"It's no problem for me to drive a tractor, Sergeant Kaminski," Zarr said.

"Everyone will have a turn driving the M-4, so we all get experience," Kaminski said. "We'll use the rotation system, like on the various positions on the Long Tom."

In September, Borys sent a letter informing Martha that he was somewhere in southern France. He indicated that before boarding the troop transport from Italy to France, he had a shower— the first hot shower he had in months.

As always, he expressed his passionate feelings for Martha. Borys felt lonesome for his "Sweet Heart" as he lay awake at night for hours thinking of her "in different countries on different continents."

As September closed, mail call was greeted with great fanfare, since contact with home was slow. Borys received two letters: one from home and one from his brother Alex.

The first letter Borys opened and unfolded was from his parents, which they had sent the previous month. His father, Paul, was distraught.

Paul had planted some crops—mainly corn, potatoes, and tomatoes—in his victory garden. Some crops were ripening, and he planned to start harvesting them soon.

When Paul went to the garden, the crops were gone. He swore it must have been a German spy who had stolen them since no honest fellow American would stoop so low!

Alex, the youngest brother, wrote that he had gotten a few vegetables out of his victory garden several blocks from their home. He shared them with the family, which calmed down their father a bit.

Borys sent this V-mail letter home on September 13, 1944, from "Somewhere In France:"

Dearest Mother,

This is my first letter I'm writing you from France. Also just wrote
Martha a Vmail. It'll take a week or so before I catch up in writing

to everyone. All by me is fine, and pray the same for all at home.

Hope you got my picture I sent from Italy. Had quite a bit of rain today, but it's cleared up now. Will write to Andy during this week. I imagine the weather is getting cool back there.

France is a nice country. Plenty of trees, and the people are clean. It's the best country I've seen overseas. I believe soon I'll see you all. Perhaps by Spring of this coming year.

How are Helen and Louise enjoying school, and how is Steve? I hope Andy gets home soon.

Will write again shortly. I expect to get a lot of mail shortly for it should catch up to me.

Love to all the family.

Your Loving Son,

Borys

Mid-September saw the US First Division close on Aachen, Germany. The US First Army struck at the Siegfried Line in the Aachen area two weeks later. Now that the Allies were in Germany, it appeared the war would end by Christmas 1944. The GIs would soon go home!

The Allied bomber offensive against Nazi synthetic oil production reduced output substantially from the second quarter to September 1944. German aviation fuel production also decreased markedly during the same period. Synthetic plants produced almost half of the German fuel for vehicles and nearly all the aviation production of the country.

25

OCTOBER 1944

Marseilles, France

On the western front, the Germans had the protection of the steel-reinforced concrete Siegfried Line to prevent incursion into the western part of the fatherland.

The Allies had more than twice the artillery as the Germans, but the Nazis had more mortars. The Allies had a temporary logistics supply problem with their artillery shells due to the necessity of transporting war matériel through limited harbors. Also affected by this momentary constraint was gasoline, which was in short supply, a shortage shared by the Germans because of the Allies' intensive and successful bombing campaign of Axis oil supplies.

The Allies dominated the Western European skies with nearly fourteen thousand aircraft, compared to fewer than six hundred German aircraft on the western front. The remaining Luftwaffe aircraft—fewer than four thousand—were in other European countries.

A breakthrough of the first portion of the formidable Siegfried Line north of Aachen, Germany, occurred on 7 October. The second portion of the Siegfried Line east of Aachen remained intact.

The Allied advance across France and into Germany gave hope of the war's end by Christmas 1944; Borys was one of the millions who wished it so and expressed that to Martha:

Dearest Beloved Martha,

While over here I only hope you're happy and well for I can't help worrying over you Dearest.

There isn't much I can do for you Martha Darling while I'm over here so I can only say if you need anything or see anything you like, don't hesitate to get it, for I know you Darling just as if you are [my] wife and I want to make you as happy as possible while I'm away.

I still expect to surprise you sometimes this year and I'm just going to hug and love you so that you won't even have a chance to straighten your beautiful hair....

Darling, I want you to make a big roast dinner when I get back but don't make it too good for I'm liable to faint eating my first good meal in a long time....

I'm the lucky one to have fate give me a girl like you Darling. If I'd have never met you Beloved, my life would still be empty and lonely, now that I have you Darling to share our hardships, our love and our happiness, to work for our home and our own little family, I feel now that I've everything in this life to work hard for.

I think of when we have our own home of the laughs and fun we'll have. I picture you sleeping next to me, cooking and caring for our house, going out together to a show or restaurant and always being together. Gee Martha Darling that's the only thing I'm look-ing for....

*I'm only praying to have the blessed day in church with you Be-
loved, to become my wife. I often picture you Darling in your Bridal
Gown next to me and the both of us saying "I Do".... The day is
coming Beloved Mine when I'll have you in my arms to kiss and
love as my wife.*

*I may even decide to give you an extra kiss... as you know me
Darling, you'll never see me hesitate to give you an extra kiss. As a
matter of fact you're going to get thousands of extra kisses from me
and I'll never stop once I'm with you Dearest again....*

*I miss your sweet kisses and love but the memories of your love
are deep in my heart.*

I Love and Adore You, Martha My Own Dearly Beloved Darling,

Borys

Two 62nd AAA Battalion enlisted men were presented with Soldier's Medals. These
GIs had entered a heavily mined area to administer first aid to a fellow soldier wounded by an anti-personnel mine in Marseilles, France, on 18 October 1944.

During the 1944 World Series, the Saint Louis Cardinals, representing the National
League, defeated the Saint Louis Browns of the American League in four games to
two. After the war, the Browns moved to the East Coast and became known as the
Baltimore Orioles. In the lesser-known "Kiss Series" between Martha and Butch,
Martha was ahead with 50 kisses owed her by Butch; he lagged with only 25 kisses
owed him.

26

November 1944

Marseilles, Épinal, Saint-Dié, and Strasbourg, France

During their occupation, American troops discovered that fall is the rainy season in France's Lorraine and Alsace regions. September, October, and November each averaged three inches of rain; however, November 1944 was more than double the average, with almost seven inches of cold, soaking downpours. November's inundation caused rivers to reach flood stage and the second-rate dirt roads to become swamp-like terrain as army tanks, trucks, tractors, and jeeps attempted to navigate them.

On 11 November, Armistice Day, a two-minute silence was observed at 1100 hours by all battery formations to honor those lost in the Great War.

Reaffirming his love for Martha, Borys wrote:

My Own Dearly Beloved Martha,

I'm praying I get some mail today Darling....

After I'm out of the army and working, we're going to do a lot of shopping to pick furniture and all the things that we'll need for our home.

Then when we're married Beloved and have our furniture, but before this we'll have to pick our place to live so that it can get our furniture set in, and then get married and go on our honeymoon, we'll be already or have our home ready to live in.

What do you think of it this way Beloved?

What I've lacked in sending you gifts from over here, I'll do my best to make up to you some day Beloved.

Martha Darling, forgive me when I take you in my arms when we're together again because I'm going to hug you, kiss you and love you until I'm exhausted....

I'm writing now that the sun has come up and its cold in the morning. You must still be asleep and I wish I could have breakfast with you.

Just think of when we're married Martha Darling, I'll have to sleep with you, love you, and work for you and Patrica and eat with you. I'm just going to love that and then life will really be worth living for....

A lot of changes have taken place, and every day going by is a day nearer when I can be with you again Beloved.

I hope the war can't last to much longer, for if it does I'll have white hair when I get back to you. Believe it or not Darling, I haven't a gray hair yet, but quite a few of the boys have been getting gray hair. Well Darling, I guess I'll always be young.

There's nothing I'd want more on this earth than to be with you Beloved before the end of this year. Although I've been pretty busy... I was always lonesome for you Martha Darling, for anyone or anything could ever fill the space in my heart that you've filled Beloved....

With all my Undying Love to you Martha.

Loving You Forever Martha My Beloved, Only Yours,

Borys

Borys expressed Thanksgiving blessings to Martha and her family. He was saddened that this was the third Thanksgiving that he and Martha would not share, as they were separated by the vast expanse of the Atlantic Ocean. Instead, he had to settle to look at one of her pictures and reminisce about the times he had held her and kissed her with longing, yearning to hold her again. Borys knew in his heart that the happiest Thanksgiving he would ever have would be the first one he shared with Martha.

The battalion received orders to report to the Seventh Army in Épinal for assignment. Movement of the battalion from Marseilles began on 14 November.

Confidence was building that the war's end was near—the mess trucks of each battery led the motor convoy to the bivouac areas for the GIs to have a hot meal upon arrival. This was small compensation to GIs who were skin-drenching wet from the cold, continuous, typhoon-like showers with accompanying pitch-black darkness.

When the 62nd AAA reached its destination, the inside of the small pup tents they set up had the disagreeable odor of wet wool from their uniforms and blankets. The sound of pounding rain hitting the outside canvas tents and surrounding ground with ponding puddles was audible throughout the night and slowed to a drizzle as daybreak approached. With first light, the rain stopped, the artillerymen packed up, and continued their motor convoy.

The 62nd AAA Battalion arrived in Épinal on 17 November and the 90-mm M1A1 guns fired at road junctions in case of enemy movement and responded to red alerts, thus breaking German aircraft formations and preventing casualties and damage to matériel.

Commencing 19 November, multiple red alerts sounded daily as German reconnaissance and fighter aircraft flew overhead, day and night. The battery left Épinal-based positions on 24 November to occupy sites in the area of Saint-Dié.

In *As I Remember It: The War Years 1940 – 1945,* John Manning, the author and Battery C Commanding Officer during the war, tells of an incident at a French farm. One of the GIs shot a cow, and, in the spirit of teamwork, other Battery C personnel pitched in to slaughter the bovine. That night, the soldiers had steak dinner, which they shared with a company from the 3rd Infantry Division on the march.

The following day, an officer from the Army's Criminal Investigation Division (CID) stopped by Captain Manning's tent. The farmer was wise to the carnage involving the livestock in the pasture and filed a complaint with the US Army.

The CID officer informed Manning that the farmer accused his unit of killing and stealing his cow. He further stated that the Frenchman was seeking compensation for the pilfering. Captain Manning said he would make payment, in French francs, from the battery's Welfare Fund to satisfy the situation. With agreement from the CID officer, payment was made, and the incident closed with the agreement of all parties; the farmer received fair restitution, the CID promptly closed the case, and the artillerymen (along with the infantry company) had a fresh, hot meal rather than cold rations from a can—a true win-win situation.

On 25 November, the battalion was relieved from attachment to the VI Corps and proceeded to Strasbourg, occupied by the French Second Armored Division since 23 November 1944.

A clap of thunder sounded as the 62nd AAA Battalion sloshed its way along the muddy rain-swept road. Along with the pounding rain came more lightning and thunder. With each flash of lightning in the night's darkness, the men could see vehicles heading in the opposite direction.

At a crossroad, they saw an MP directing the other convoy's traffic—a German MP!

Neither of the opposing forces chose to battle. All soldiers realized there would be a bloodbath with no winner on the road; neither side had the advantage of surprise, position, or overwhelming force.

The farther the American convoy drove, the thinner their German counterpart became until it ebbed entirely, leaving an open, muddy road. The 62nd continued toward its destination, which they hoped was unoccupied by Axis forces.

All batteries were ready for action by dark on 26 November.

Unknown to the GIs, the Germans went south to Colmar, France, as the Americans headed east towards Germany and the Rhine River, which the soldiers in the German convoy probably realized.

In the vicinity of Strasbourg, several gun positions were under intermittent German small arms fire from both the east (front) and the west (rear). Fortunately, there were no casualties.

The Strasbourg bridges were defended on one side by American antiaircraft guns and the other side by German antiaircraft guns. However, the Free French had warned the Americans not to fire since the Germans would retaliate by bombarding the Strasbourg city power plant. Reluctantly, the 62nd AAA Battalion complied with their host's request.

November saw the GIs receive mummy-type sleeping bags to use instead of two blankets. Fortunately, the soldiers wisely kept both, since the coming winter would prove brutally cold. In fact, the winter of 1944/1945 was the coldest on record in Northern Europe since the beginning of the century. To stay warm, the antiaircraft artillerymen's bodies would burn more calories than they consumed, resulting in significant weight loss.

27

DECEMBER 1944

Strasbourg, France

The US campaign bombing German aircraft-manufacturing plants and aircraft-fuel supplies was so successful that Allied bombers were attacked by few German fighters in the summer and early fall of 1944. To counter the Allied campaign, the Germans scattered plane manufacturing to more than seven hundred small factories rather than the original twenty-seven large factories. Consequently, Nazi slave laborers built over three thousand fighters in September 1944.

The second half of 1944 saw an intense bombing campaign against German oil and transportation targets. By the New Year, Nazi synthetic oil production was under seven percent and aviation fuel production under three percent, compared to earlier in the year. Fuel shortages in Germany were at a catastrophic point. The Third Reich's shipping, rail, and road transportation were reduced by more than half, which resulted in the inability to supply vital materials for production; 20 percent of the German labor force was needed to remove rubble from bombings and to man antiaircraft weapons.

The December days grew shorter and the nights longer, to as much as sixteen hours. The previous month's rainstorms and fog turned to sleet and snow, blanketing the battlefield landscape before Christmas.

Their woolen uniforms did not provide enough warmth against the bitter freezing temperatures, which reached below zero Fahrenheit in late December 1944 and January 1945. The intense icy cold caused thousands of cases of trench foot.

Multiple red alerts were sounded from 1–9 December, day and night. Hostile aircraft, flying at low altitudes, raided the Strasbourg area and attempted to drop supplies to isolated German troops. Hundreds of rounds of 90-mm and .50-caliber ammunition were fired daily to prevent injury to Allied personnel and damage to materiel; two enemy aircraft were destroyed in early December.

Harassing and destructive fire on enemy artillery, railroads, and road junctions continued throughout December, with thousands of field artillery rounds fired at German targets. Additional red alerts from 10–31 December resulted in three enemy planes destroyed, two probables, and two damaged.

The German counterattack in the Belgium Ardennes Forest on 16 December is referred to as the Battle of the Bulge because of the deep penetration, or "bulge," into the American lines. At its greatest point, the Bulge measured approximately sixty miles wide and fifty miles deep in the Belgium/Luxembourg area of the US First Army.

This was an inhospitable battlefield, with blankets of snow covered by rock-hard ice. The woodlands consisted of white forests, and all waterways had thick, glassy surfaces.

With an appalling disregard for human life, a new Nazi army had been raised using elderly German men, boys in their midteens, foreigners from German-occupied countries, and personnel from other branches of the Nazi military as well as experienced army groups. The army would make a swift infiltration using hundreds of new panzers into southern Belgium and the northern portion of Luxembourg. In addition, German commandos dressed in American uniforms and with US dog tags from captured and dead GIs committed sabotage behind American lines. They gave incorrect directions to infantry and armored units, including changing road signs and cutting telephone lines, causing as much havoc and damage as possible.

Although the Germans made significant progress in the first week of the Battle of the Bulge, when the cloud-covered skies cleared over the Ardennes region on 23 December, ten thousand Allied aircraft went on the attack.

The German salient was short-lived; in January, the Allied armies attacked the Nazi armies and pushed them back the miles the Germans had gained in mid-December.

Borys sent Christmas greetings to Martha, her family, and his blessings for the New Year and above all, peace in the New Year, 1945. The 62nd Antiaircraft Artillery Battalion produced a Christmas card for the soldiers with a poem inside; Borys sent one home:

Tho throughout the globe I may roam,

My every thought is still of home.

No land could ever quite compare

To the Christmas' we used to share.

So I am sending here to you

A wish I make, may it come true.

The next will be-

A very merry Christmas

and a Happy New Year

-with you.

28

JANUARY 1945

Strasbourg and Morhange/Colmar, France

From the war's perspective, the 62nd AAA Battalion started the New Year off well with destroying one enemy aircraft and damaging two others between 0130 and 0230 hours on 1 January 1945. On New Year's night, the battalion fired on enemy ammunition dumps and antiaircraft guns.

The German Operation Northwind was an attack in the Alsace region to reduce the likelihood of American reinforcements going north to the Ardennes area. This is where the main German Battle of the Bulge offensive occurred in Belgium.

The Nazi objectives under Northwind, commencing 1 January, were to sever US supply lines and to capture Strasbourg.

As the day closed on 2 January 1945, Battery C received orders to move from Strasbourg to a new location about thirty-five miles away. French officials protested the American departure as a political and military mistake. They wanted the Americans to return to Strasbourg to prevent German retribution against loyal French citizens. On 3 January, the US forces were instructed to hold the Maginot Line and under no circumstances give up Strasbourg.

Upon reaching their new location, the battery received instructions not to dig in. Less than an hour later, the 62nd AAA Battalion was ordered to reverse the two-hour drive back to Strasbourg, with orders to arrive at dawn.

Daylight broke as the antiaircraft artillery trucks entered Strasbourg. House after house, street after street, improvised white flags made from pillowcases and sheets, decorated windows and doors.

"Jesus Christ," Lake said. "There's got to be twice as many surrender flags as there were French flags last night."

"They're afraid of the Nazis, and they're just trying to survive," Borys said.

"Son of a bitch!" Pollock yelled as he drove the tractor.

"Look," Borys said, pointing a finger at a Nazi flag hanging from a window.

"Son of a bitch," Kaminski said. "I'm not letting that bastard get away with that. Pollock, lean on the horn. If we can't sleep, neither can a Kraut sympathizer."

Less than thirty seconds later, the window opened, the German flag was yanked in, and the gun crew drove on with its horn still blasting, causing a chain reaction of horns forming a sonata of protest.

The following day, Kaminski shared some news with his men. "The French military arrested the character with the Kraut flag in his window. Justice has prevailed."

During 6–10 January, multiple skirmishes broke out in which 62nd AAA batteries came under enemy artillery fire. The batteries returned thousands of rounds of defensive 90-mm counterfire.

The battalion was instructed to move to the vicinity of Morhange on 10 January. For the next two weeks, the battalion would fire harassing missions at roads and road junctions used by the Germans. They also commenced fire on German batteries and patrols.

The January temperatures were ten or more degrees below zero Fahrenheit and rarely warmed to the freezing point of water at thirty-two degrees in the afternoon.

Caught in Nature's arctic-like freezer for weeks, the artillerymen discussed their situation: "Unfortunately, there's less than ten hours of sunlight in January and far too much darkness," Goldman said. He pointed in the woods and said, "Hey, look, here comes Kaminski with a replacement crew so we can have our turn in the warming tent."

"I'm going to the truck to get our food," Pollock said. "I'll meet you in the tent."

After updating their situation to their replacements, the gun crew entered the warming tent.

"Boy, oh boy, that feels good," Goldman said as he opened the door to the stove and tossed more coal into its belly to fire it up.

"Mind if I back into that baby?" Lake asked. "The cold is wreaking havoc on my bones."

"Sure, help yourself," Goldman replied as he moved aside.

After a minute with his back toward the stove, Lake said, "Thanks, that felt good. Next!"

With the temperature forty to fifty degrees warmer in the tent than outside and still warmer—even hot—by the stove, the men took turns at the heater.

Just then, Pollock entered the warming tent with cans of warm rations retrieved from the tractor's engine compartment. "Here, everybody grab one."

"Thanks. It's your turn at the stove, Bob," Borys said.

As the antiaircraft artillerymen started eating army chow, Pollock said, "Hey, Butch, I'll trade you my dessert for your crackers and cheese."

"You got it," Borys said as they traded rations.

When they finished their meal, a howling wind outside reminded everyone of the intense frigid weather they were soon to face again.

Zarr said, "Even with two pairs of socks, two sets of trousers, two shirts, a combat jacket, an overcoat, gloves, mittens, and the stove, I'm still cold."

"How cold does it get in the city?" Pollock asked.

Lake answered, "The coldest was on February ninth, 1934, when the temperature got down to minus fifteen. I remember it because we had no heat in our flat, and my mother was freezing when I got home. I brought her to a friend's bar, which was nice and warm; he'd just opened it since Prohibition had ended two months earlier."

"Rumor has it this is the coldest winter Europeans have seen in their lifetimes," Borys said.

"Well," Zarr said, "the Germans on the other side of the Siegfried Line are just as cold as us and maybe even colder."

"Time's up!" came a yell from outside the tent. "Everyone out!" The occupants were forced to make a reluctant exit.

The last week of January 1945 saw field artillery missions involving an antitank position, a command post, a mortar position, a factory occupied by enemy troops, railroads, roads, and road junctions.

On 28 January, the Germans were anticipated to use the next few moonlit nights to strafe Allied positions. The newly received M51 Quad .50-caliber machine guns were to be fully manned at night as well as in daylight hours.

On 29 January, a group of six German Me 109 airplanes attacked Allied sites. The AAA Battery .50-caliber machine guns damaged two low-flying enemy aircraft.

The American bomber campaign against German oil facilities since April 1944 caused a fuel drought for panzers during the Battle of the Bulge. The Nazis anticipated capturing US fuel supplies in the Ardennes Forest, but American aerial attacks after the cloudy weather cleared turned the tide of battle.

29

Morhange/Colmar, France

The cold weather continued in February, albeit not freezing much of the time. Temperatures generally ranged in the mid to upper-thirty-degree range. Continual rain and melting snow turned the frozen earth into a quagmire. GIs were the main targets in Old Man Winter's sights, drenching them first in rain and then mud, even on their weeks-old bearded faces. This ferocious character would bring cold weather and even snow flurries until the end of April before the lovely Spring Maiden made her welcome appearance in Europe. Yes, soon winter would pass just as the Third Reich's final moments approached.

Late in the afternoon on 1 February, Battery C arrived in Ban-de-Laveline, France, where the residents invited them into their homes, grateful for the restoration of liberty the Americans brought with them. Borys, Pollock, Goldman, Lake, and Zarr were assigned to a large home occupied by a couple in their late forties to mid-fifties. The couple asked them to take a bath in hot water. Zarr, standing with a stunned look on his face, caused the woman to inquire if she had insulted him.

"No, madam," Zarr said and then asked, "You mean there's still hot water on the face of the earth?"

Borys apologized for tracking dirt into their home and started to explain that they had been in the field for months. The couple interrupted him and said no explanation was needed, for the entire town knew and sympathized with the soldiers' plight; that's why they were pleased to have the troops spend the night in their warm homes.

Borys could now sit down and write Martha; he had been negligent in this respect the past month due to continued combat and movement to multiple locations. Borys asked Martha not to worry if she didn't receive his mail for long intervals because he would be back to love and adore her. He also told her that he was safe and reminded her of their tradition regarding the Blue Danube Waltz on their special day, 25 March. Letting Martha know he was well was most important—he even forewent asking her for candy, especially chocolate, since it would not melt in the cold weather.

Borys was highly appreciative of the hospitality offered by the French—it reminded him of the elderly French couple in Oran, Algeria, who treated him like a son. He hoped the battery would stay in this cozy hamlet at least a few days; his expectations were dashed as the battery moved the following morning. His forethought in writing Martha proved fruitful as she received the V-mail and played the Blue Danube Waltz, as was now their custom. Furthermore, Martha was comforted knowing Borys was safe, at least in early February.

On 2 February 1945, the 62nd AAA Battalion arrived in the Colmar Pocket. Each battery took a position in a different town. The battalion drove off enemy aircraft three times that afternoon, with no Allied casualties or damage to matériel.

From 4–8 February, Battery C fired on roads, road junctions, and a bridge west of Neuf-Brisach used by the retreating German troops. Other batteries received orders to move to the vicinity of Colmar.

Death and tragedy hit the 62nd AAA: German artillery struck the Headquarters Battery, killing a lieutenant and severely wounding a technical-sergeant major from the 253rd Radar Maintenance Team on 6 February 1945. They were immediately sent to an evacuation hospital at Saint-Dié. Because French First Army headquarters planned to occupy Colmar, the 62nd AAA Battalion moved back to its earlier positions on 8 February 1945.

The eleventh of February brought a letter of commendation from Major General Frank Milburn to the battalion for "the superior manner of performance in the operation of clearing the Colmar area."

Although Borys found it extremely difficult to write Martha the opening months of 1945, Martha continued to correspond with him faithfully. On Wednesday, 14 February 1945, she wrote Borys a Valentine's Day letter:

My Dearest Beloved Sweetheart Borys,

This time it's a letter during my lunch hour and not a V mail from a fe-male. Did you ever hear of that saying? It's not the exact words, but something similar to it.

Darling, didn't write you last night because I just couldn't get down to writing. Either the baby bothered me, Lizzie had the radio on etc. So I listened to the radio for a while and went to bed. It seems like a habit with me – always in bed sleeping. You're going to have your troubles with me when you marry me.

It's still snowing out. Doesn't get a chance to let up, it seems that way. The way things look as though it will snow all summer. Doesn't bother me in the least – nothing does any more. – Just like a Zombie.

I asked Catherine (Kitty) if she got any mail last night. "No" was the answer. It seems to be that most of the time. I should know better not to ask and the reverse.

One of the girls (General assignment) is leaving for "Cadet Nurse" today, so we are going to have a little party for her. The usual way, as though it were a birthday. Cake, and present the person with a gift. We got her a fountain pen because she needs it.

I don't recall mentioning to you that I bought myself a brown pair of shoes. Was going to wear them when I went to West Va. I needed a pair anyway. Just a plain shoe, all closed, with a little bow in the front. People admire them. Boy it's difficult getting ones size. Mine 5¼, usually get 5½.

Martha's brother George had been critically shot in December during the Battle of the Bulge. George was evacuated to England and then sent to the United States. Martha and her mother traveled to West Virginia to visit George in a government hospital while he recuperated. Borys later determined that the 82nd Airborne Division, in which George served, was committed to the northern portion of the Battle of the Bulge near Trois-Ponts. He already knew George had received a lesser wound at the Anzio beachhead early in 1944.

The top of my head hurts from all the bobby pins (to keep down that mop of mine).

Up to the present day, I haven't received the photos you sent from France – if you sent it.

Today is pay day and you can see it by the looks of the club room. No one is here, all out shopping. I would like to buy some things myself but I have to save the money and buy some food for Wednesday

(Feb. 21) because we're having a hen party at my house. It's my turn to invite them. Four of them, including myself is five. Anna, <u>Catherine</u>, Rena, <u>Connie</u>. We were to the underlined already for supper, we leave right from the office. Dance, play games etc. Strictly Women! What would I do if you came in unexpected? Crash it, Huh! Would I love that. The reason why I picked this day, for the next day is a holiday (Washington's birthday) and we can sleep late. Wasn't I smart?

Almost forgot Darling, today is, "Valentine's Day." Sending you my Beloved, all my love this day and always.

God Bless You!

Take Care!

You have my undying, unlimited Love forever.

Your Sweetheart,

Martha

In February, the 62nd AAA Battalion had its first encounter with a German jet. The screaming roar of skyward engines caused gun crews to react to the threat posed by the enemy aircraft and instinctively take position at the AAA gun.

Because of its low-flying level, which thwarted radar detection, and the surrounding terrain, which supplied cover, the jet flew unimpeded.

Since the jet had targeted no Allied position, the belief was that it was trying to intimidate the Allies with its speed. However, over the next few months, the only actual military intimidation on display was the speed with which the Allies conquered Germany.

The natural obstacle formed by the Rhine River presented an extremely difficult challenge to the Allied armies. The Rhine has a fast current and runs between six and twenty feet deep. This barrier later delayed the 62nd AAA Battalion on its western bank for about a month, providing protection at troop crossings against marauding Luftwaffe aircraft.

PART FOUR:

GERMANY AND HOME

30

Mᴀʀᴄʜ 1945

Morhange/Colmar, France, and Dirustein and Hofheima, Germany

From 1–19 March, the 62nd AAA Battalion fired field artillery missions in France and Germany consisting of a neutralization barrage of German entrenching operations, the pounding of roads and road junctions, the firing of volleys of shells at enemy troops in woods and buildings, the use of counterbattery fire against Nazi artillery positions, the cannonade of a German command post, and the bombardment of retreating enemy soldiers crossing a bridge. One enlisted man was awarded a Purple Heart for wounds received from enemy mortar fire.

Because of continued battle and movement by the 62nd AAA, there was no correspondence from Borys to either his darling Martha or their families. This included sending Easter greetings, which fell early the following month, on 1 April 1945.

The thirteenth of March saw the movement of half the 62nd AAA Battalion into Germany, with the rest moving to new positions within France but closer to the German border.

The twenty-first of March brought instructions to move to temporary positions. From that day forward, the 62nd AAA Battalion would expect to occupy sites for a day at a time without revetments. Daily movements continued through the rest of the month.

Allied aircraft dominated the skies and provided fighter and bomber support. The Germans would soon sacrifice their dwindling air power in a futile attempt to stop the Allies.

On 24 March, one enemy plane commenced bombing and strafing about two hours after sunset. The following night, two enemy planes were engaged.

The twenty-sixth saw ten hostile planes engaged between 0122 and 0407 hours; four were removed from the sky, as were two more the following day.

The remainder of the 62nd AAA Battalion crossed the Rhine on the evening of 27 March—the final great barrier in western Germany. One of the nice little courtesies of the army engineers was a pontoon bridge to traverse the water obstacle.

The battalion traveled approximately ninety miles the last week of March. All 62nd AAA batteries were in Germany; most of the battalion was on former Nazi territory for over half a month.

The CO of the Fifth AAA Group sent a letter of commendation to the CO and personnel of the 62nd AAA Battalion for their splendid service from 11 January to 24 March 1945. The CO of the 23rd AAA Group sent a letter commending the 62nd AAA Battalion on its part in successfully protecting the Rhine crossing.

The Allies were on the move, cutting like a surgeon's scalpel into the cold black heart of Nazism to remove its malignant tumor. The Allied armies were moving fast and furious deep into Germany. As March began, US forces were pressing forward at eight to ten miles per day on the Cologne Plain between the Siegfried Line, near the French border, and the Rhine.

The end of March saw the Allies take the industrial Saar region and poised to capture the industrial Ruhr region. Allied forces were now deep in Germany. The race was on to take as much Nazi territory as swiftly as possible.

Americans knew that their armed forces were crushing the Third Reich under the wheels of their trucks and jeeps and the treads of their tanks. Allied navies had destroyed the German navy, and their planes had bombed entire cities with industrial areas into rubble. The world knew the Thousand-Year Reich was crumbling fast; as the Western Allies advanced east and the Red Army headed west, the twain would meet.

As March neared its close, a long-anticipated mail call brought Borys sad news from Martha—her brother Johnny was killed on 23 February.

John Boretsky received the Silver Star. US Army documentation stated, "… while engaged in photographing the erection of a bridge across the Roer River in the outskirts of Duren, Germany, he was killed instantly when struck by enemy mortar fire. For the gallant manner in which he performed in action against the enemy on this occasion, the Silver Star was awarded to him posthumously."

From 1941 to late 1944, Johnny was in an antitank company of the Forty-First Armored Infantry Regiment of the Second Armored Division. Because he was a photographer before the war and wanted to get recognition for his photographic experience in the service, he requested and received a transfer to the First Army's Eighth Infantry Division, Photo Detachment F, One Sixty-Fifth Signal Photo Company.

After the war, John Boretsky's body was disinterred from the US military cemetery at Henri-Chappelle, Belgium, and brought back to the United States. He was buried in New York on 22 November 1947.

31

April 1945

Wattenheim, Gernsheim, Weipertshofen, Donaualtheim, Schwabegg,
and Landsberg Concentration Camp, Germany

The Allied strategy was to quickly capture as much of Germany as possible before the Nazis could set up mountain defenses in southern Germany and Austria.

For months, the fuel shortage plagued the Wehrmacht and became more severe with each passing day. Germany was desperately low on fuel in April, which hampered the use of their remaining panzers, trucks, and other vehicles as the full effect of the Allied strategic bomber offensive settled in. Nazism was in a state of collapse.

The first half of April saw the 62nd AAA Battalion fire on hostile aircraft, including a twin-engine Me 262 jet, although it flew too fast for confrontation with AAA flak or .50-caliber contact. Additionally, the 62nd AAA Battalion continued to defend the Seventh Army's Rhine bridges.

President Franklin D. Roosevelt died on 12 April 1945. Vice President Harry S. Truman was sworn in as the thirty-third US president that same day.

By mid-April, several Nazi concentration camps had been liberated by Allied forces.

Battery B destroyed an enemy aircraft on 18 April.

On 21 April, a commendation arrived from General Dwight D. Eisenhower: "Supreme Commander's Order of the Day, 20 Apr 45 commending members of the Sixth Army Group for their part in the destruction of the German forces west of the Rhine and for the crossing of the Rhine."

Between 22–26 April, the 62nd AAA Battalion moved to the Danube River; the antiaircraft artillerymen were to provide field artillery support.

On 24 April, Batteries A and C engaged twenty-nine enemy aircraft defending the Dillingen Bridge during ten raids in small groups. They also fired hundreds of artillery shells at roads and road junctions that day and the next.

On the twenty-sixth, Batteries A and C engaged two enemy aircraft. One enlisted man was awarded the Purple Heart for the wound received during this air raid.

On 28–29 April, the 62nd AAA Battalion captured and assisted in apprehending and guarding approximately three thousand German soldiers.

The countdown was continuing to Allied victory and world peace. The passing of each day brought the world closer to the war's end.

It was obvious to Americans from newspaper and radio reports that the Third Reich was now a second-rate nation in its death throes. It had sadly earned the dubious distinction of the number one murderous regime in history.

The last days of April also brought the last thing on earth the 62nd AAA Battalion GIs wanted to see—a German prison camp near Landsberg, a Dachau subcamp, with hundreds of dead. Most of them had been nearly dead from starvation before being put to death by the prison guards. An estimated twelve thousand prisoners died in the camp of hunger and sickness caused by diseases that had been prevalent among the inmates in the eleven months it had been open. They had been forced to work in an underground aircraft plant as slave laborers.

Battery C fired on two Me 109s with their M-51 .50-caliber machine guns on 30 April. In the town of Bobingen, occupied by one of the batteries, the Germans were instructed to feed a group of malnourished displaced persons first and then German townspeople only after the freed slave laborers had eaten. Orders came as 30 April closed: the battery was to move out to a new location farther into Bavaria.

32

MAY 1945

Seeshaupt, Schwabmünchen, and Altenstadt, Germany

Major news arrived on 1 May about the Nazi hierarchy: Adolf Hitler was dead. Before his death, Hitler had appointed Grand Admiral Karl Doenitz as his successor.

Battery C knew it would be just a few weeks before the end of the war in Germany.

The few remaining German planes only flew reconnaissance missions now. Orders came to relieve the battalion of its antiaircraft artillery mission. All heavy guns, fire-control equipment, and two of the four M51 .50-caliber AAA guns were to be transported to an airfield south of Augsburg for storage, where guards would remain with the equipment. Two M51 .50-caliber machine guns were to remain for local defense.

Information led to a German general hiding in Bobingen, who had stored valuables in a town rayon factory. He was arrested and taken to the factory, where an AAA battalion squad searched the building. Former French laborers who had been forced to work there assisted in looking for valuables. Thousands of silver ingots were found in an air raid shelter room. Behind a freshly cemented wall in an underground room were nozzles made of gold palladium, used in making rayon thread. Almost a ton of precious metals were removed and transported to the military government at Schwabmünchen.

Effective 2 May, the battalion's mission became a security role, with each battery securing a town. Battery C arrived in Seeshaupt at the south end of Lake Starnberg, near Munich, at midday on 3 May 1945.

The Seeshaupt train station contained railroad cars filled with dead bodies on the way to the Dachau crematoria. The area immediately adjacent to the train also had bodies that had fallen from the train. They had landed there when live people, essentially consisting of skin and bones, had dug their way out of the body masses to escape. The train's SS guards had abandoned the station and train when the Americans approached.

On 6 May, the 62nd AAA Battalion assumed control of POW camps at these locations:

- Batteries A and B: camp at Gauting, with 20,000 POWs
- Battery C: camp at Schwabmünchen, with 6,800 POWs
- Battery D: camp at Altenstadt, with 8,400 POWs

The seventh of May brought the news the world had waited for—Germany's unconditional surrender. Initially, the surrender was signed in Reims, France. Soviet Premier Stalin insisted that it be held in Berlin for Soviet ratification. Consequently, 8 May became the official Victory in Europe Day (V-E Day), with the surrender ceremony held in Berlin that day.

With the capitulation of all German armed forces in early May, security became the major issue. German soldiers surrendered by the hundreds of thousands; AAA battalions were to provide security to contain the POWs until they could be discharged. Thus, from 8 May 1945 to the end of June 1945, the primary mission of the 62nd AAA Battalion was to guard and administer POW enclosures.

Borys reminisced about Martha's birthday three years past when he proposed marriage. With this on his mind, peace in Europe presented the opportunity for Borys's final poem to Martha; it honored their lasting deep love and was dedicated to the young woman he adored. He wrote it to reach Martha in time for her birthday:

I see a vision of you before me,

Though we're apart across the sea,

I've memories to cherish of love so true,

My heart pours forth its love to you.

The vision of your tears is not in vain,

In the darkest of hours our love will never wane,

The vision of your smile will never fade,

For it is a smile that God had made.

The endless waves of the ocean blue,

Carry the message of my love for you,

Your vision shines like a light from above,

And in that vision I see our true love.

As time passes by our love draws nearer,

As the days go by the vision is clearer,

Our love not in vain but honest and true,

Just as the night I parted from you.

We'll meet again sweetheart someday,

Our love cannot be divided and will find a way,

In the darkest of hours if things seem blue,

Remember Martha Darling, I'll always love you.

Additionally, Borys wrote that due to the harsh winter, he had lost weight. He optimistically stated, "Don't worry Darling, that makes it easier for you to put your arms around me to kiss." He added that every time he looked at Martha's pictures, he became "lonesome for your love and keep longing to have you in my arms," because, "Martha Darling, I love you and adore you."

Borys believed the army would soon send him home and discharge him. Thus, he would have Martha's companionship for her twentieth birthday the following month. He expected to give "my personal birthday wishes along with scores of kisses."

33

JUNE 1945

Altenstadt and Kornwestheim, Germany

On 1 June, the battalion received orders to construct a POW camp in Kornwestheim, Germany, to house seven thousand SS officers and noncommissioned officers.

Lumber, nails, and wire turned into prisoner barracks and fences. After the camp was completed, the first five hundred internees arrived on 16 June 1945. In processing the SS, the following procedure was used:

- A physical search was conducted of each man, including his clothing and equipment, and all field equipment was confiscated; any item that could be used to commit suicide was collected.
- Soap and a towel were issued to each man for showering.
- Each man's clothing was deloused.

Once the internee stated his name, he was issued a number, mess gear, and a blanket and was assigned to a room. Then, an identification card was issued, all valuables were turned in and a receipt given, and each man received a haircut and shave (under the supervision of guards) upon arrival at the barracks.

On 20 June 1945, the 62nd was relieved of its mission to guard SS POWs and was placed in strategic reserve. A point system was instituted for demobilization to send men home. Points were given for time overseas, duration of service, and combat decorations. Anyone with eighty-five or more points was eligible for demobilization; like Borys, most men in the 62nd AAA Battalion had 135 points. The men complained that they wanted to return to the States, for they had defended Britain and had fought in North Africa, Sicily, France, the Rhineland, and Germany. It was now someone else's turn. The battalion was told they would become replacements in other units returning home to expedite their departure from the European theater of operations.

The end of June saw the breakup of the 62nd AAA Battalion, with men transferred to other outfits. Borys was reassigned to the 533rd AAA Battalion.

A letter arrived from Martha in the last mail call before his transfer. She complimented her "Sweetheart" for the birthday poem and good wishes:

> *...the poem you wrote was wonderful and such an imagination....*
>
> *Sweetheart, you have nothing to fear because I kept my promise always to be true to you....*

Borys responded:

> *Martha Darling, it was simple for me to write the poem, I just had to picture or see your vision before me and the rest was easy.... I only tried to express my love for you in my humble way.*
>
> *I know you will always and forever be true to me and it isn't because you promised me, but because we love each other and our love and trust for each other will never die.*

Even amid a devastated Germany, where a birthday present was impossible to find, Borys managed to write Martha:

I Love and Adore You Martha, My Own Dearly Beloved Darling,

I was thinking to have at least one week for our honeymoon, and I believe I may surprise you Darling with something on our honeymoon, for lacking to give you a gift on this birthday....

I miss your love, your sweet kisses, your smile, our arguments, my sleeping and snoring on your shoulder in the theatre, and Darling I guess you miss my sleeping on your shoulder in the show.... Just as you're my sweetheart now Darling, you'll always be in years to come after we're married.

I Love You now Martha Darling, just as great or greater than the Day I asked You to become My Wife.

I place you above, Martha My Dearly Beloved, and have you above anything on Earth knowing your love for me is as great.

Smile Darling and keep smiling for I Love You, Martha My Beloved Darling.

Loving You Now as Always and Forever Will,
Borys

34

JULY 1945

Germany

Borys arrived at the new AAA battalion on Monday, 2 July 1945, and was assigned as a radar operator. The nature of the assignment did not matter to Borys, since he was going home soon. As he thought of home and his darling Martha, Borys composed the following:

My Own Dearly Beloved Martha, My Darling Love,

I've received no mail since I left my old outfit....

If only I would have known you wanted to take me in your arms and squeeze me the night we had a date and I waited in the snow, I would have taken you in my arms instead, but only I didn't know how you would take it.

After we found out we loved each other we didn't care who was around. Do you remember your little sister Lizzie used to get disgusted when I'd kiss you in the parlor and she'd leave? I used to get a kick out of Lizzie. Tell her that was the way we could have the parlor to ourselves. Tell her we'll buy her an ice cream soda for taking the hint and leaving us by ourselves. Also I'll be back this year to treat her to that soda.

Gee Darling, how I loved you then, just as I do now and forever will love you Martha Darling.

...all the kisses you gave me are still lingering in my heart and will always linger in my heart.

Life to me would be worthless if I didn't have you Darling. You filled the empty place in my heart when I met you Martha Dearest.

We'll have each other soon Darling, our love, our home and our own little family.

God Bless you Darling and all the family.

I send all My Undying Love to You Martha, My Beloved.

My Love, My Darling Martha,

Borys

Scuttlebutt had it that Borys's new outfit was being held for the invasion of Japan. That would be one tough and bloody job. The army needed experienced men to fight the Japanese, and they fit that category. It seems the point system had a loophole to exclude those considered vital for war duties, and the battalion fell into that loophole.

Further news of fighting in the Pacific came everyday to those awaiting discharge. The news was terrible, as casualties mounted with each offensive—the Philippines, Iwo Jima, then Okinawa.

Indoctrinated Japanese soldiers committed fanatical suicidal attacks against American marines and GIs on Okinawa. At sea off Okinawa, the Japanese used the kamikaze not only for individual attacks on naval vessels but also in large groups. Some of these suicide raids included as many as three hundred aircraft.

Because waves of kamikaze planes assaulted the US fleet continuously, more men and ships became casualties at Okinawa than in any other battle fought by the US Navy. The nearly 10,000 US Navy casualties at Okinawa represent approximately 15 percent of the total US Navy casualties in World War II. As a result of the roughly nine thousand sorties by Japanese aircraft (about three thousand, or one-third, were kamikaze sorties), thirty-six US Navy ships were sunk and 368 were damaged. The Japanese lost over seventy-eight hundred aircraft.

Okinawa became the most deadly battle of the Pacific theater, with over 12,500 US combat fatalities and more than 36,600 wounded. The Japanese lost approximately a hundred thousand men and, because of a large civilian population, over 150,000 inhabitants of Okinawa.

Early in the morning of 16 July 1945, the United States detonated the first atomic bomb at Alamogordo Air Force Base, New Mexico. The blast was heard as far as a hundred miles away and was visible 180 miles away.

Because of the increasing ferocity and desperation of the Japanese in their assaults on Americans, the growing concern was that the number of American lives lost by invading Japan would be astronomical.

President Truman gave his final approval for using the atomic bomb on Japan.

35

Aᴜɢᴜsᴛ 1945

Germany

The first five days of August were uneventful except for the anticipation of being shipped overseas to the war in the Pacific. Mail call brought letters from home, finally! Borys received several, including one from Martha, wishing him a happy birthday, albeit days late. As he read Martha's older letters, he worried they might get lost in their travel to the other side of the globe. To prevent their disappearance, he immediately started sending small groups to the States each week to ensure at least some would be safe.

Borys reaffirmed his love for Martha:

My Own Dearest Beloved Darling,

As I once wrote you Darling, the bitterest day and moment of my life was when we parted... I kept looking as New York harbor was slipping past the boat and was staring toward Brooklyn.

Some day soon I pray, I'll see NY Harbor come toward the boat I'm on so I can see you come toward me Darling, and that day I know will be my Darling.

...Darling you're the only one who has given me happiness without looking for something in return, with the exception of my Love of which you never will lack to have and which you now have and always will. No one Beloved could ever give me what you've given through your heart to me.

What you've offered to become my wife for the love of me, and to bear my children through you Beloved, no other human could offer me more than what you offer through your love for me. No Darling and my Beloved Martha, again I'll honestly say no one but you... could ever or ever have treated me better than you Darling....

My love for you Martha Beloved will always be, and as long as your love for me exists which I know always will, no one will ever come between our love, of which we have all the right in this world to cherish and possess for each other.

You remember Beloved the nights I kissed you and the nights we spent for loving each other. And the night I proposed to you, knowing our only thoughts were of marriage to always be together to share our love and happiness in our own home.

I know I'll always be happy with you Darling..., we'll love and plan our lives, and plan our children's life and future so that they may have a better start in life. You'll notice I've said "children's", so Darling I suppose it'll have to be more than one...

I love you with all my heart, Martha Dearest.

Dearest Darling Loving You Always Forever,

Borys

On 6 August 1945, Armed Forces Radio announced the use of an atomic bomb to destroy a Japanese city, Hiroshima. After three days, another Japanese city, Nagasaki, was destroyed by an atomic bomb.

GIs felt sure that the destruction of Japanese cities would bring the war to an end. Although they realized thousands of civilians were killed, the soldiers were relieved that it now appeared the Japanese would be forced to surrender and, in the long run, both Allied and Japanese lives would be spared.

At noon on 15 August 1945, the Japanese Emperor Hirohito Showa spoke on the radio for the first time: He announced Japan's surrender. Due to the time difference across the International Date Line, it was still 14 August in the United States.

Although Japan had surrendered on 15 August, the articles of surrender were not signed until 2 September.

36

SEPTEMBER 1945

Germany and Fort Devens, Massachusetts

Borys waited with great anticipation for news to go home. It came on 2 September, from his commanding officer. With the signing of the official Japanese surrender, the battery would fly home the next day. All personal possessions must be immediately discarded. Only the clothing the men were wearing was allowed on the plane due to weight restrictions. Every unnecessary ounce was ordered to be destroyed. An officer would come back for inspection in one hour.

The battery busied themselves with dumping unnecessary items.

As promised, the men were called to attention for inspection one hour later. They had retained letters, pictures, articles of clothing, war souvenirs, liquor, and other personal effects. The lieutenant making the inspection waited and watched as men were ordered to line up and throw any "excess baggage" in the trash.

Borys had to discard all Martha's letters, including her Valentine's Day letter from 1943.

That was the letter in which Martha had expressed how lonely and empty her heart had become with Borys's absence.

That was the letter Martha had kissed with red lipstick and Borys had kissed every night, even after he'd worn all the lipstick away.

That was the letter Borys so cherished that he always kept it in his breast pocket, close to his heart.

That was the letter that broke Borys's heart as, with great reluctance, he hesitantly placed his valued correspondence in the trash.

The only solace Borys received was knowing that this act would get him on a plane to America. A plane to bring him home soon to Martha. The plane trip across the Atlantic would take less than a day rather than more than a week by ship. More time to spend with Martha.

The following morning, 3 September, the battery was told their plane trip had been delayed until the next day. Borys thought of all that had been thrown away. He then reflected and found comfort in a philosophical viewpoint: "Throwing everything away from the past three and a half years is symbolic of putting army life behind me and advancing into civilian life."

Borys walked, thinking of his comrades from the 62nd AAA Battalion and with visions of Landsberg Concentration Camp. He had mixed emotions: Borys was pleased when thinking of his fellow artillerymen but melancholy when recalling the horrible sights of the slave labor camp; it was something never to be forgotten. Borys continued walking until he reached the Red Cross, where free postcards were distributed to military personnel to write home. He asked for two: one for home and one for Martha.

Borys thought that with the airplane flight, he would be home before the postcards, but he would write them as souvenirs for the families. He wrote to Martha, short and sweet:

> *I'm writing the three words you longed to hear for more than three years.*
>
> *"I'm coming home"*
>
> *I'm closing with the words I have most sincerely written you these same years:*
>
> *"I Love You."*

To his parents, he wrote to tell them and his siblings he would be home soon.

On 4 September, orders were given to pack all gear and personal effects. The battery followed this order immediately— all their personal effects were already gone.

A shadow of gloom settled over the 533rd as they loaded into trucks for transport to the harbor. Harbors meant docks, docks meant ships, and ships meant no planes and one to two weeks at sea.

Borys arrived back in the United States on 13 September 1945. At Fort Devens, Massachusetts, on 19 September, he was discharged. At the separation center, he received $100 mustering-out pay (and was owed $200 more) and $1.90 travel pay. Borys's battle and campaign records on his discharge included: Algeria, French Morocco, Rome, Arno, southern France, Rhineland, and Central Europe.

After the war ended, housing shortages continued to plague the nation, particularly among returning veterans. Martha and Borys, caught in the housing shortage, were forced to move in with Martha's parents in Brooklyn, New York. Many other veterans also found moving in with relatives preferable to living in cold-water flats, huts, or even tents.

Their first child was born about nine months after they were married in 1946. Because they were living with Martha's parents, whose names were George and Anna, they named their first child Georgianna rather than Patricia Ann. It was not until 1947 that Martha and Borys found an apartment of their own; during the same year, rationing in the US stopped. Their second child, also a girl, was born in 1950, and they named her Christine. The following year, their last child, James was born. It appears Martha took Borys's advice from a letter he had written to Martha in May 1943:

... As far as the number of children we'll have Darling, after we're

ahead, we'll let nature take its course. Martha Darling if we let na-

ture take its course, my God, we'll have an army. You'll have to put

a limit on me Darling, for I'll never know when to stop.

In 1951 Martha and Borys bought their home in Brooklyn.

After his honorable discharge from the US Army, Borys worked in the printing industry as a stereotyper/electrotyper, a trade he retired from in 1980.

Borys fulfilled his plans to marry Martha, have children, raise a family, and buy a house, the American dream. Martha and Borys celebrated their fiftieth wedding anniversary in Brooklyn with their three children, other family members, and friends on 20 January 1996. He passed away seven months later and Martha, in April 2003.

ACKNOWLEDGMENTS

First and foremost, I would like to extend my gratitude to the men who served in the 62nd Anti-Aircraft Artillery (AAA) Gun Battalion. They were part of the Greatest Generation; a generation, who, at the time the world around them was crumbling, reinforced the 18th century foundation of freedom that America's forefathers built. Through their sacrifices, they made the 20th century United States the greatest nation known to mankind. To me, the most important members of that era were my parents, Borys and Martha Bohun, who shared their love and devotion through more than a half century of successful marriage.

I also have a special word of appreciation to other family members, who provided encouragement or material while writing *A Soldier At War: The World War II Letters of Borys Bohun.*

Additionally, I am indebted to William Harbaugh, Commanding Officer of Battery A, and John Manning, Commanding Officer of Battery C, 62nd AAA, during the Second World War. Bill Harbaugh provided me with a copy of *The War Diary of the 62nd Anti-Aircraft Artillery (AAA) Gun Battalion* (it is my understanding that Bill researched the 62nd AAA at the National Archives and developed this document), photographs of the battalion, and information during our conversations. John Manning also provided me with information during our talks and a copy of the book he wrote, *As I Remember It: The War Years, 1940 – 1945.* John's book was a valuable source of material for my book.

I express my gratitude to the following World War II veterans of the 62nd Anti-Aircraft Artillery Gun Battalion and/or their spouse for their written contributions:

Andrew Borix; Harold Clark; Conception Conti; John M. Godfrey, Col. USA (Ret.); Edward Hogan; Lawrence A. Komoroske (Larry also contributed photographs); Carol and Ken Meuse; Ruth and Herbert Schloz; Frank Orski; Merwin Patterson; Edward Poje; Ed Snyder; Evelyn and James Towne.

Lastly, I would like to thank Cheryl Hanna for the colorized photo of Borys on the cover.

ABOUT THE AUTHOR

James Bohun, a native of New York, graduated with highest honors from the City University of New York with a bachelor's degree in history. He began a career in government and worked in federal service for almost nine years, then worked for the City of New York for over twenty-seven years. Subsequent to retirement in 2015, at the age of sixty-five, Bohun moved from New York City to Tampa, Florida, where he researched, wrote, and completed this book. He is a member of the Authors Guild.

WWW.JAMESBOHUN.COM